HIBIS... ...TAL

Nurse Rennie Phillips grabs the opportunity of sailing round the world as nanny to the Carmichael family—the ideal way to cure a broken heart. But a call at the island of Tavalei shatters her new-found calm. The hospital there is run by Dr Craig Mackenzie, the one man she is trying to forget. Her feelings are as strong as ever, but can she ever forgive him for the way he deceived her in the past? Tavalei holds only the prospect of renewed heartbreak for Rennie, so why is she so reluctant to leave?

HIBISCUS H⊙SPITAL

Hibiscus Hospital

by
Judith Worthy

MAGNA PRINT BOOKS
Long Preston, North Yorkshire,
England.

British Library Cataloguing in Publication Data.

Worthy, Judith
  Hibiscus hospital.
  I. Title
  823(F)   PR9619.3.W6

  ISBN 1-85057-203-8
  ISBN 1-85057-204-6 Pbk

First Published in Great Britain by Mills & Boon Ltd. 1982.

Copyright © 1982 by Judith Worthy

Published in Large Print 1988 by arrangement with Harlequin
Enterprises B.V., Switzerland.

Printed and bound in Great Britain by
Redwood Burn Limited, Trowbridge, Wiltshire.

CHAPTER ONE

'Rennie! Brett! Andy!'

Peta Carmichael's voice drifted up from the galley, and a moment later she appeared at the top of the companionway. 'Lunch!' she shouted, then vanished again.

Rennie Phillips, who had been half asleep, stretched her slender bikini-clad, sun-tanned body and languidly rolled over. Her slightly wavy hair, already bleached to a creamy gold by the sun, scarcely stirred in the light breeze that was carrying the yacht along at a steady rate over the deep blue, white-capped Pacific.

'Come on, imps!' she said, drawing her knees up, ready to get to her feet, and smiling at the two young children in their bright yellow life-jackets and harnesses. 'Lunch time!'

The calm weather had allowed Damien and Emma to become absorbed in a serious game involving building blocks, and for once they were reluctant to be disturbed even for food.

'I am so lucky!' Rennie said to herself yet again. The children were certainly no trouble to look after.

She untethered the harnesses from a stanchion and shepherded her charges along the deck towards the companionway. The aroma of macaroni cheese drifted up appetisingly from below. Peta was a wizard cook and turned out delicious meals without fuss, as though she was at home.

Rennie had met Peta and Brett Carmichael in New Zealand only a few weeks ago, but already they were like old friends. It had been a fantastic chance for her, hearing that they were desperately looking for a nannie for their two children aged four and three. They were sailing around the world in the yacht *Spindrift*, and their nannie had left them suddenly because her boyfriend had cabled from London that he wanted to get married.

What a fabulous thing to happen, Rennie had thought enviously when she heard about it. She didn't blame the girl for flying home straight away. Absence had certainly made one heart grow fonder, it seemed, and one girl was lucky in love. If only she could have been too, if only Craig...

Swiftly she crushed the thought of him as it surfaced again now. Craig Mackenzie must be forgotten—*must, must, must*. It was pointless even thinking about a man who was married.

She had done the right thing getting out when she had discovered it. Perhaps she had over-reacted, dashing off to work her way around the world, but she did not regret it, especially not now.

During the past two years she had worked in hospitals in the Middle East and in Africa, had done private nursing and relieving work in Australia, and in New Zealand she had worked in a private clinic, a children's hospital, and recently as a nurse to a spastic boy in Wellington while his mother was in hospital for an operation.

It had been Mrs Kitson who had heard of the Carmichaels' plight and who had recommended Rennie. Although it was not a nursing job, Rennie had jumped at the chance of sailing with them. She knew nothing about boats, she had told them, doubting they would want to take her, but they had said they would soon teach her.

In the few weeks she had been with them, Rennie had learned quickly, mainly because Andrew Barker, Peta's younger brother and Brett's partner in a boat-building business back in England, who was travelling with them, took it upon himself to spend every spare minute teaching her. Now she was nearly as useful a crewman as any of them, he said. Rennie knew this was flattery, but nevertheless she felt pleased with her progress, as she had often dreamed it would be, going to sea in a sleek white yacht was an experience she would not have missed for worlds.

Andrew reached the companionway as she and the children were about to descend. He looked down at her from his considerable height, blue eyes twinkling with laughter and a quirky twist to his mouth. He was a redhead like his sister, and ruggedly good looking. As Rennie smiled at him, she hoped her tan would conceal the warmth she felt flowing into her cheeks.

Andrew had kissed her last night when they were on watch under the stars, with the phosphorescence foaming away from the sides, the moonlight dancing on the dark water rushing away from the yacht's side, and above them the rhythmic creaking of the rigging. There was no reason for embarrassment now and she felt none, but she did feel slightly uneasy. She was not sure she ought to let a romantic relationship with Andrew develop, even if it only lasted the voyage, and yet...her heart argued that a little harmless flirtation might help to erase the memories of Craig which running away had only made stronger and more painful.

'I'd better take a look at your hand present-ly,' she said, matter-of-factly. He had cut it rather badly two days ago when splicing rope, across the palm from little finger to between index finger and thumb.

'What would I do without you,' he mur-mured, and as the children, released from their harnesses, scurried below, he followed close behind Rennie. He ran a finger lightly down her bare spine, tweaking the strap of her bikini top playfully. She turned her head to glare at him, but knew he would not take it seriously. She hoped he wasn't going to prove a problem. She was very conscious that in the close con-fines of the yacht, over a period of months the slightest difficulties in relationships would be magnified.

Brett came down behind them, having put the yacht onto auto pilot. 'Perfect day,' he remarked, as they all slid into their places on the benches on either side of the table. 'But it isn't going to last. There's a low developing right on our course according to the last forecast I picked up.'

Peta looked up anxiously from ladelling out helpings of macaroni, and Rennie, too, glanc-ed at him as she stowed the children's life-jackets out of the way, to see if he was con-cerned.

He grinned at them. 'No need to look so worried, you two! I didn't say it was a gale warning!' He added, 'And as we're more or less outside the cyclone season, there's no cause for alarm.'

'Brett, don't?' cried Peta, setting his bowl in front of him. 'Just the thought of a cyclone makes me go all weak at the knees.'

'It'd be a good test of your seamanship,' said her husband relentlessly, with a wink at the others.

Peta handed the rest of the bowls of macaroni around and playfully slapped her husband's cheek. 'Give over, Brett! Do you want to scare Rennie?'

Rennie pushed the dish of parmesan cheese across to Andrew and caught his eye. He was looking at her in a speculative way, and when their knees accidentally touched under the table, she drew hers back abruptly. On so small a vessel it was inevitable that they all came into some sort of physical contact practically all the time as they moved about the tilting decks and the confined space below, but what had up until yesterday been casual and inconsequential contact now, after last night, seemed to have significance. The thought of cyclones did not make Rennie nearly as uneasy as what she saw in Andrew's eyes.

Brett laughed. 'I bet Rennie would revel in it!' He was fond of teasing Peta. This was her first long sea voyage and although she was an accomplished yachtswoman, previously all her experience had been in fair-weather conditions and near to land. They had struck a few storms on the way from England to New Zealand, the worst being in the Great Australian Bight, she had told Rennie, but although she hated storms she revelled in everything else about sailing, and according to Brett, never panicked. They were very much in love, Rennie had realised almost immediately, totally in tune with each other, and she envied their easy-going but profound relationship.

After lunch Rennie renewed the dressing on Andrew's hand. Unlike two days ago when the accident happened, and she had attended to it with the impartiality she would have shown to any patient, today she was acutely aware of him as a man, and there seemed to be an intimacy about changing the dressing.

'It's a nasty wound,' she said, 'it really needs to be stitched, but there are no sutures in the first-aid box, unfortunately.'

'I bet you're a dab hand at sewing!' joked Andrew.

'Only in emergencies,' said Rennie, adding with a smile, 'and some sutures don't need a

15

needle and thread!'

'You can see the doctor in Tavalei,' put in Brett, who was poring over charts on the table. 'We'll be there tomorow morning if the weather holds.'

'I'll be okay,' said Andrew, as Rennie fastened the end of the bandage.

He joined Brett at the table, and Rennie put the first-aid box away and started the washing up. Peta, who had been settling the children for their afternoon nap, merged from the cabin and joined her.

'Did I hear you say we'll definitely be in Tavalei tomorrow?' she asked, taking up a teatowel.

Brett looked up at his wife, still teasingly. 'God willing and the wind fair!'

Rennie paused with her hands in the washing up water, strongly aware of the rhythmic rolling of the yacht, the jerk as the auto pilot continually brought them back on course. This was sailing at its best, a good wind, a sea that was comparatively calm, and cloudless skies. She hoped the low up ahead would move quickly away and not bother them. She didn't want any crisis to spoil the serenity of the voyage.

Presently, she and Peta, having completed the chores that needed to be done, including the washing which now flapped like a row of flags across the after deck, stretched out on the deck to sunbathe. The children were still asleep below and the men were in the cockpit. It was unbelievable, Rennie thought, being paid for enjoying herself like this. Her duties consisted mainly of keeping an eye on the children when Peta could not, giving them some very simple lessons more to amuse than to educate, and doing whatever other tasks she was delegated on the boat.

'I wonder what Tavalei will be like,' murmured Peta. 'I gather it's more unspoilt than some of the other South Sea islands. There are about fifty islands in the group, so Brett said, but only about half a dozen of them are inhabited. Tavalei is the largest.'

'And evidently quite civilised,' said Rennie, watching the big spinnaker bellying in the wind as though it could not get enough of it. 'Brett said there was a doctor.'

'Yes, and a hospital I beieve,' said Peta. 'And one hotel. It's becoming quite a popular tourist spot apparently, but there's no international airport or anything like that yet, and the harbour isn't suitable for cruise ships so only small vessels like ours, and schooners or luggers can dock there.'

'How do the tourists get there?' asked Rennie. 'Not all in their own yachts presumably.'

17

'No. There are a couple of schooners doing charters, and there's an infrequent seaplane service, and that's all at the moment.'

'It sounds idyllic,' said Rennie. 'I'm looking forward to it, aren't you?'

Peta yawned. 'You bet I am.' She sighed happily. 'You know, Rennie, I thought Brett and Andy were crazy wanting to sail *Spindrift* around the world. I thought it was irresponsible taking the kids along, so young, but now it's happening, and we've already sailed half way, I can't imagine why I ever demurred!' She laughed suddenly. 'To think that if I hadn't let them persuade me I'd be sitting at home in Southampton now, biting my nails and wondering what was happening to them.'

Rennie smiled understandingly. 'You mean it's better to weather the storms in reality instead of in imagination?'

'Exactly. Even though the first storm we struck was sheer hell for me. I was convinced we would sink. We didn't of course, and most of the time I was too busy helping the boys to think of the danger. Anticipation is always the worst part of anything nasty. Nevertheless, I hope we're going to miss any bad weather that's about. Andy's a bit restricted with that hand.' She glanced across at Rennie. 'Although you're a pretty useful sort of sailor now, if we

18

have an emergency.'

'I'm crossing my fingers we don't,' said Rennie. 'I don't yearn to be put to the test.'

Peta sighed. 'We were lucky to find you, Rennie, but I feel a bit guilty really.'

'Why, for heaven's sake?'

'Well, it's a bit of a come-down for a nurse, just being nannie to a couple of brats, and spare deck hand!'

Rennie laughed. 'I wouldn't have come if I'd thought of it like that. To me it's the opportunity of a lifetime.'

'Well, it's reassuring for us,' said Peta, 'to have someone like you with us just in case we do have some medical crisis.'

Rennie gazed up at the sky, the billowing sails, the straining rigging, and thrilled to the swift rushing of the little white boat across the ocean beneath her. They were hundreds of miles from land, a mere speck on the limitless blue ocean, little larger than a foam crest on a wave. It was humbling, she thought, and exhilarating.

Peta had dozed off but Rennie's mind was too active for sleep, despite the warm sun's soporific effect. That Andrew, who had so far regarded her as just another crew member, had suddenly and subtly changed, continued to disturb her. She liked him a lot, although he

19

was perhaps a little too casual, too inclined to treat everything lightly. But he was good fun, as well as good looking. The trouble was she wasn't sure she wanted a romantic involvement with him.

Rennie was on watch again that evening with Andrew. They shared the night watches in pairs. Previously Rennie had not minded sharing the darkness hours to midnight, or midnight to dawn, with Andrew. They had talked a lot, played chess and found plenty of tasks to do. She had been learning all the time about sailing, and Andrew was a thorough teacher.

'Wind's getting up,' Andrew remarked, as Rennie stepped down into the cockpit.

She stowed the thermos of coffee where it would not fall over, and looked up at the sky. There were ragged clouds scudding across the stars. The moon was not up yet.

'What was the latest forecast?' she asked.

'That low is still hanging about,' he answered, 'but there was no gale warning.' He was standing facing into the wind and he breathed in deeply. 'I reckon we're in for a bit of a blow, though, and some rain. I can smell it!'

Rennie laughed. 'You sailors!'

He sat down beside her, and although in the darkness she could not read his expression

20

clearly, when he said softly, 'Rennie...' she drew back instinctively.

'Aren't there things we ought to be doing?' she said.

His arms captured her, closing tightly around her. 'I can think of one thing...' Rennie resisted him rigidly. 'Rennie...what's the matter?'

'Nothing.' She tried to shrug his arms away, averting her face.

'I thought you liked me.' He sounded hurt.

'I do...' She turned back to look at him and her heart was beating fast. She said slowly, 'But I don't think...well, it's a very small boat...'

He was laughing softly. 'Peta and Brett won't object to a little romance! Peta's hell bent on match-making anyway.' He pulled her firmly back into his arms and his mouth was on hers before she could turn her head again.

His lips moved against hers with mounting passion, and although something deep inside her stirred and responded to his physical contact, it was against her will. It made her angry to realise that her struggle was as much against herself as him. His hands were fumbling under the sweater she wore, warm and caressing on her bare skin, sliding up and down her spine. When she felt him deftly slip the hooks on her brassiere, she jerked back convulsively,

21

resisting him easily only because he was now not expecting her to.

'No! Andrew, please...'

His hands were already moving forward, and she grabbed them through her thick sweater and prevented them straying any further. Andrew looked at her in puzzlement for a moment, then realising she meant it, he rather sheepishly withdrew his hands.

His mouth twisted in a crooked smile. 'Naughty boy!' He slapped the back of his good hand with the bandaged one.

Rennie had to laugh. 'Oh, Andy, you...!'

'It's all right,' he said, only a shade surlily. 'I get the message.' He looked at her steadily for a moment. 'But you might have said first there was someone else.'

'Someone else...' she was startled.

'You don't fool me,' he said drily, 'even though I try to fool myself. I know when I'm kising somebody who would rather be kissing someone else.'

Rennie was startled. She had not expected such perception from Andrew. 'I wouldn't rather...' she faltered, knowing it was a lie. She added quickly, 'I...I'd just rather we kept things as they were...before...'

He regarded her quizzically. 'Either you're lying, or trying to fool yourself as well as me.'

He took her hand. 'Somebody let you down badly once, is that it?'

Rennie saw it as a way out. 'I don't want to talk about it,' she said, pulling her sweater down hard around her slim hips.

'Fair enough, but brooding over him won't help, will it? If there's no chance, I mean?'

'There's no chance,' she answered dully, a familiar ache tightening like a band around her heart.

'Was he the reason you scarpered out of England to work your way round the world?'

She nodded.

'I thought there had to be a reason. You're not really the kind who's adventurous at heart.'

'As you are?' she said with a smile.

'He laughed. 'There's plenty of salt in my blood, I suppose.'

He put an arm around her, comfortingly this time, and she did not object, knowing he would not try to take advantage now. He said, 'Sorry I moved too fast, but...' His face was close to hers and he was looking at her with unconcealed desire. 'You are quite irresistible!'

Rennie felt uneasy again. 'Andy...I hope this isn't going to spoil things,' she said hesitantly.

'Spoil things? Why should it? Man makes pass at girl, girl rebuffs him. Back to square one. No hard feelings, Rennie. I can take it!'

Rennie was not sure that he could. 'We'll still be friends?' she ventured.

'Mates!' he averred. 'Shipmates. You're turning into a first-class seawoman, Rennie, and I wouldn't want you complaining to the skipper, and jumping ship at the next port because I've offended you. Promise you won't do that? Good crew are hard to find.'

He looked really worried, so Rennie reassured him. 'No, I won't do that.' Nevertheless she wondered how the months to come would be. They were a long way from home and she was determined not to let Peta and Brett down. They had already been let down once. Nor did she want to quit *Spindrift*. She was very happy sailing with the Carmichaels and Andrew, if only Andrew...She heaved a sigh. Perhaps it would be all right.

Andrew pulled the chess set out of the locker and they played for a while, but both were too preoccupied to play well. Finally, Rennie won the game. She said, 'I didn't deserve to win that, Andrew. You weren't concentrating. Let's have some coffee.'

They were sipping the coffee and munching biscuits when a figure suddenly emerged from below. It was Peta. Rennie glanced at her watch. It was not yet time for changeover.

'Rennie, could you come below for a minute?'

Peta asked, in a low, anxious voice.

'What's the matter?' Andrew asked, sensing her agitation.

'Is it one of the children?' Rennie was scrambling up.

'No, it's Brett. For the past hour he's been having some sort of attack, like colic, he says, but Rennie, I'm sure he's in considerable pain...' She peered closer at them both. 'Are you two all right? I thought at first it must have been something we ate, but I can't think what. We all had the same, and the fish was what Andy caught only this afternoon.'

Rennie said nothing. There were a number of things that might cause the sort of pain Peta had described. She followed Peta down to their cabin forward of the galley. The children were fast asleep in their specially railed-in bunks, and Brett was lying rigidly on his, his face white and strained.

'He's vomited quite a bit,' said Peta.

Rennie went swiftly to his side. She lifted his wrist and, resting his arm across his chest, felt for the pulse. Then she asked him about the pain, where it was situated, how frequent the spasms were. He said it seemed to be shifting from the centre of his abdomen to his right side, which confirmed Rennie's strongest suspicion.

She turned to Peta. 'It looks very much like appendicitis, I'm afraid.'

'Appendicitis!' Peta gasped. 'Oh, no!'

Brett murmured shakily, 'My conclusion exactly, Rennie!'

Peta covered her face with her hands. 'It would have to happen now.'

Rennie fought down the panic she was feeling herself in the face of this crisis. 'Brett,' she said, 'we'll be in Tavalei tomorrow, and there's a hospital there, so it's not as bad as it might have been.'

Peta rallied at once. 'Of course not, darling! We should be entering the channel at first light. You'll be in hospital by breakfast time!' She held his hand tightly and he smiled wanly at her.

Rennie was thankful they were so close to a landfall. There was precious little she could do in the circumstances, except give Brett a sedative. The only cure for his condition was an appendectomy as soon as possible. She took his temperature. It was slightly up, but nothing to be alarmed about yet. After she had given him a sedative she turned to Peta.

'You stay with him, Peta, I'll tell Andrew and we'll take the second watch too. There's nothing we can do, except get to Tavalei as quickly as possible. Call me if he seems feverish or there's any other change.'

She said that more to reassure Peta than with any specific notion of what she might do. Peta smiled gratefully, her face pale and anxious in the dim cabin light.

As Rennie ran back up the companionway, the yacht lurched suddenly and she fell against the handrail, clutching it to steady herself. As she emerged on deck the wind seemed fresher than before and when she got back to Andrew and told him about Brett he grimaced.

'Looks like we're in for a rough night one way and another. Wind's getting up, and the barometer is falling fast. We're heading straight into bad weather.'

'Is there any way we can avoid it?' Rennie asked.

'Not unless we sail right off course, and there's no guarantee we will even then.'

'We must get to Tavalei in the morning,' Rennie said.

Andy looked at her. 'How bad is he?'

'He's critical. We must get him to hospital as quickly as possible.'

Andrew nodded grimly. 'I'll do my best. There's no point in reaching the Tavalei group before dawn though. We need daylight to see our way in. There's no pilot. We have to find our own way through the shoals.'

'Is that dangerous?' Rennie asked, thinking of Brett out of action and Andrew with an injured hand having to cope alone.

'Not if you know what you're doing. I'll need both you girls probably, at least for part of the time. We don't want to run aground or hole up on a coral reef. Tavalei is a tricky entrance according to the book, and as we haven't done it before, we'll have to be doubly careful.'

'Just tell me what to do,' said Rennie.

'Right now,' said Andrew, 'I should make some more coffee. You'll be too busy presently, I suspect, for anything so mundane, and we may need something to revive us later.' He added, 'I'm going to batten down just in case.'

Rennie went below again to do as he had suggested. She did not want to alarm Peta so she just mentioned it in passing, saying she thought she would be glad of a hot drink presently. But Peta was not fooled.

'Andy's reducing sail,' she said, 'which I take it means we're heading into rough weather.'

'I think it's just a precaution,' said Rennie, checking that the guard rails on the children's bunks were securely in place, so that if the yacht began to pitch and roll violently they would not be flung out. She was glad they were in the same cabin with Brett and Peta so that

Peta could keep her eye on them.

She stowed one thermos of coffee, together with some bread rolls Peta had made earlier in the day, in the cabin; the other she took up to the cockpit. There were few stars visible now, and the moon which had risen gleamed whitely only now and then behind the fast-moving banks of cloud that had suddenly piled up. A few spots of rain spattered onto her face. Like Andrew and Peta, she put on her life-jacket.

It was two a.m. before they ran into the storm. It was almost with a sense of relief that Rennie greeted the howling wind, the massive seas. She knew now what Peta had meant earlier when she had talked about the anticipation being worse than the reality. Once you were in the storm you were too busy keeping your wits about you to be afraid, and your thoughts, if you had time for any, were not fearful anticipation any longer, but the certainty that eventually the worst would pass.

Andrew was considerably hampered by his injured hand, but at the height of the gale Peta joined them, calm and efficient and rising to the occasion just as Brett had said she did. Rennie was full of admiration for them both, and the way they handled the yacht. There were times when the seas rose, it seemed, to mast height before crashing down on them, and

Rennie was sure they would be splintered to matchwood. Every time there was a brief lull either Peta or Rennie would rush below to see how Brett was and if the children were all right. Brett was sleeping fitfully and at first seemed unaware of the storm. Once, when Rennie went below, Emma had woken, crying, but she soon soothed the child back to sleep. Damien slept soundly despite being tossed about his bunk.

On deck, buffeted by the gale, lashed by chill needles of rain, Rennie discovered that she was not afraid, only awed by the fury of the elements, and filled with admiration for the tenacity of the fragile craft that dared to defy them. Whatever Andrew or Peta ordered her to do, she did without question.

She did not notice at first when it began to grow lighter, but suddenly she realised she could see the others more clearly, as they huddled in the rain-soaked cockpit, watching and waiting for the next cruel gambit of the wind. Their faces told of the strain of the long dark night. Quite suddenly the wind almost dropped.'

Rennie reached for the thermos in the lull. 'Coffee?'

'I'll just slip down and see Brett,' said Peta.

'We're through the worst,' said Andrew, his grip on the wheel slackening. Rennie heard his involuntary wince of pain as he took the cup from her in his injured hand, and she noticed the bloodstains on the bandage. He had evidently wrenched the wound open again.

'I hope so,' she murmured, exhausted and yet exhilarated too because they had won through.

In another hour, the wind had abated to a steady blow and the rain had cleared. The seas were still high and shards of cloud scudded low across the sky, almost at mast height it seemed to Rennie. Spray still lashed the decks and when Peta came up with mugs of steaming hot thick soup, Rennie realised how chill she had become, and that she was soaked to the skin.

'You'd better change into dry clothes,' Peta said firmly, 'or you'll be in hospital too. You too, Andy.'

Rennie obeyed. She went to see the patient first however. He was awake and although he maintained valiantly that he was no worse, his face told the story of how the night had been for him with continuous nausea and pain. She checked his pulse and temperature, frowning deply. Both suddenly gave her some cause for concern. The storm's buffeting had certainly not improved Brett's condition.

'No breakfast for you,' she said smilingly.

'You'll be on the operating table in a couple of hours.'

He grinned at her. 'I'm not hungry anyway. Some storm last night?'

'Just to add to the excitement and your discomfort,' said Rennie.

'Rennie...' A small sleepy voice came from the other side of the cabin.

Rennie said, 'I don't know how they do it! They both slept through. Well, Emma woke once, but she wasn't frightened. Just a minute, darlings. Be very good and quiet, won't you, because Daddy isn't very well.'

'Have we arrived at Tavalei yet?' Damien was eager to be up and about.

'Not yet. Soon.'

As soon as she had finished attending to Brett and had changed into dry slacks and a cotton sweater, Rennie washed and dressed the children and took them out into the saloon, where Peta was preparing breakfast.

'Nothing for Brett,' Rennie said. 'They'll have to operate immediately.'

Peta turned anxious eyes on her. 'How serious is it?'

'He'll be all right so long as we get him to hospital soon,' Rennie reassured her. There was no point in worrying Peta unnecessarily, she thought, but she was concerned about

Brett's deteriorating condition nevertheless.

'You can take Andy some breakfast,' said Peta. 'I don't think he'll want to come below for it.'

The morning was clearing rapidly when Rennie emerged on deck once more. They were under full sail again and a good steady wind was pushing them along at a fair pace. Andrew looked relaxed and confident once more.

'How long before we get to Tavalei?' Rennie asked, taking a turn at the wheel while he ate his breakfast.

For answer he pointed ahead. 'We lost a bit of time during the night, naturally, but see that smudge on the horizon...that ought to be it.'

He took over the helm from her while she scanned the horizon through binoculars. The clouds had almost all drifted away and the sea was gradually becoming calmer. The sun was not yet up but the east glowed a creamy gold. Sometimes a big wave obliterated the horizon altogether, but there were calmer moments when Rennie was able to focus on the faint smudge far ahead. Not all that far ahead, she thought with relief, for them to be able to see it from so low in the water. They were nearly there.

'Wind's a bit variable,' said Andrew, downing a second cup of coffee from the flask she had brought up, 'but I reckon we'll be tying up in a couple of hours or so. I don't know how long it will take to get through the reefs. How's the patient?'

'The sooner we get him to hospital the better.'

Andrew nodded. 'All the more reason for negotiating the reefs cautiously. It'll mean a longer delay for him if we run aground.' His eyes held hers and there was open admiration in them. 'You did a grand job last night,' he said. 'I reckon you've earned your ticket!'

Rennie smiled wearily. 'I felt so inadequate. You and Peta are so competent.'

'I wouldn't mind you for my first mate,' he said softly, and then looking at her slumped figure with concern, 'You ought to snatch a few minutes shut-eye. I'll call you if I need you.'

'Why me? You and Peta haven't had any sleep either,' Rennie protested. 'I'm all right. I'll catch up later when we all do. I can't leave Peta to look after Brett and the children. She's as whacked as I am.'

'Were the kids seasick?' Andrew inquired.

'No. They're remarkable good sailors. The miracle is that I wasn't seasick either!'

'You didn't have time to think about it. Seasickness is partly psychological you know!' He touched her shoulder gently. 'Go and have

34

your breakfast, Rennie.'

Rennie went below. The children were excited about their imminent arrival at Tavalei and Peta was anxiously impatient. They all went up on deck as soon as breakfast was over. Rennie secured the children's harnesses and stood for a moment just looking at the sea. The sun was just coming up and briefly the sea gleamed like burnished copper as *Spindrift* ploughed on under full sail as though the storm had never been. There was a humid warmth in the breeze now, and ahead the smudge on the horizon was growing larger. Through binoculars Rennie could see the contours of hills, the shapes of trees and buildings along the shoreline.

'Hurry, hurry, hurry,' she kept saying to herself, worrying about Brett, but knew they could hurry no more than the wind would allow. There was not enough fuel for motor power, since they carried only a limited supply for manoeuvring the yacht in and out of port. In any case the wind was pushing them along as fast as the yacht was capable of going.

For all of them there was mounting excitement as the island of Tavalei drew closer. They sailed close to other islands, small atolls which suddenly seemed to rise out of the sea by magic, crowned with waving palm trees and ringed by necklaces of white foam-caressed sand.

'Lovely to be cast away on!' Peta remarked, her anxiety over Brett relaxing momentarily.

'Okay, crew, on watch for shoals,' shouted Andrew suddenly. 'We're approaching the passage. You take the starboard lookout, Peta, you take the port, Rennie, and yell if you see anything. All right, Rennie?'

'Yes...I think so,' she answered, staring ahead into the translucent green water.

There were buoys marking the passage into the lagoon, but Andrew said you couldn't just rely on them as it was an area of shifting shoals. Very slowly *Spindrift* glided towards the island which loomed ahead in greater detail every minute. Finally Andrew told them to relax.

'We're through!' Peta exclaimed and Rennie heaved a sigh of relief. Looking ahead she saw a small white motor boat heading towards them.

'Customs, I expect,' said Andrew. 'And probably the doctor. They said there would be an ambulance waiting when I radioed about the emergency.' He smiled fondly and reassuringly at his sister. 'Won't be long now, love.'

'I'd better go and see Brett,' said Rennie.

Peta waited to meet the doctor and Rennie heard the motor launch's engine revving as it came alongside.

'Doctor's just arriving,' she told Brett. He

was sweating now, she noticed in some alarm. She mopped his brow and took his temperature and pulse again, so that she could tell the doctor the very latest, although it was plain to anyone now that Brett Carmichael was a very sick man.

There was the sound of voices above and then steps on the companionway ladder. Rennie glanced towards the open cabin door as they came through the saloon. She heard a man's voice saying, 'Don't worry, Mrs Carmichael, we'll have him in hospital in no time.'

It was a deep resonant voice, a slight Scottish accent detectable from the way he rolled his *rrs*, and it slid straight into her heart like a surgeon's knife. It sounded exactly like Craig Mackenzie...

The doctor's large frame filled the cabin doorway. He had to stoop to enter, and for a moment Rennie thought she must be delirious, or mad. She felt as though someone had connected her to a transfusion unit and forgotten to take only a pint, and all her life's blood was draining away.

It was Craig Mackenzie and he was staring at her with the same shocked and incredulous expression as she knew she must be staring at him, both too thunderstruck to speak.

CHAPTER TWO

Rennie felt her whole body begin to tremble uncontrollably as she looked at the man standing before her. She blinked, sure she must be dreaming. It simply could not be Craig Mackenzie standing there, his grey eyes regarding her with amazement. But it was.

There was no time for personal feelings, no time even to ask what chain of circumstances had brought them to the same place at the same time. This was first and foremost an emergency, and professional duty must take precedence.

'Appendicitis?' Craig raised one eyebrow in the characteristic gesture that brought a flood of memories back to Rennie. She stood transfixed for one more second, until his words penetrated at last like a blunt hypodermic, and she pulled herself together with an effort. For the moment, at least, they must act as strangers.

'I suspect so,' she answered tentatively, 'from the pain pattern...'

'There's obviously some fever,' he said, taking up Brett's wrist.

'I just checked his temperature again,' said Rennie, 'it was...' Their eyes met briefly as she spoke, but if he was aware of her chaotic feelings in that moment, he gave no sign of it, nor any clue to his.

A girl in a blue and white uniform had followed him into the tiny cabin. She was obviously a nurse. She was a slim brown girl with black hair topped by a skimpy nurse's cap. She smiled at Rennie who could not help thinking how beautiful she was, in a serene kind of way. In some way her presence seemed to ease the terrible tension.

As the nurse moved in beside Craig, Rennie fell back. The girl probably didn't realise she was a nurse, too, but Rennie was only too happy to let her take over. She still felt shaky and not in complete control of her wits. She watched, as in a dream, as Craig methodically examined Brett, who was too groggy to make more than a few feebly joking remarks and smile stoically.

Her eyes were fastened on the back of Craig's neck and a string of irrelevant thoughts swept through her head, such as—he needed a haircut. When he asked her questions, briskly and impersonally, she answered in the same way, automatically and professionally. And then all at once she was aware of Peta, Emma in her arms, Damien peering around her, standing in the cabin doorway anxious, but reluctant to intrude.

Craig straightened up. He glanced at Rennie. 'Appendicitis without doubt. We'll have to operate at once.'

He became aware of Peta too, and smiled at her, his slow reassuring smile that gave everyone such confidence in him, nurses and other doctors he worked with as well as his patients, and which had totally devastated Rennie in a quite different way—once.

He said, 'Don't worry, Mrs Carmichael, your husband will be all right.' He looked down at Brett, who was becoming more aware of what was going on. 'Soon have you in hospital, Mr Carmichael. The ambulance is waiting on the quay.'

As he spoke there was an audible crunch, and a gentle bump which made the yacht shudder briefly. They all looked at each other, their faces reflecting their relief.

'Looks like we made it,' murmured Brett.

'Thank goodness,' breathed Peta thankfully.

'Excuse me...' Craig squeezed past her. 'I'll see to the stretcher.'

He disappeared and Rennie, feeling quite

unnecessary now that the other nurse was there to care for Brett, held out her arms to Peta. 'I'll take the children, Peta.' Peta handed Emma to her, and went to her husband's side. Rennie caught Damien's hand in hers and took them both up on deck.

'Is Daddy sick?' asked Damien.

'Yes, love, but he'll soon be better,' Rennie reassured the little boy.

She was relieved that Craig had brought a nurse with him. It meant that she was saved the ordeal of having to be with him for any length of time. Briefly, as she climbed the companionway with the children, she examined what her feelings had been in that moment of confrontation. She had often wondered how she would feel if she accidentally encountered him again, but it had seemed a very remote possibility, and nothing could have been further from her mind this morning. Her reaction had been purely spontaneous, and she despised herself for it as much as she despised him. He still had the power to make her feel as she did not want to feel—not for him. He had used her, deceived her, humiliated her, and she hated him. No treacherous physical reaction was going to change that.

Up on deck the bright sunshine almost blinded her for a moment and she blinked dazedly.

Then she saw that they were tied up at the quayside. There were other yachts fore and aft of them, and there was quite a crowd gathered on the quay. The word had evidently gone around that there was an emergency case to be taken to hospital.

Rennie's gaze hovered over the colourful group standing in solemn expectancy before her. Instinctively she smiled and waved her hand in greeting. Immediately all their faces broke into broad smiles and a dozen hands waved back in friendly fashion.

'What's the trouble?' A stout Polynesian woman in a colourful cotton dress came closer.

'Appendicitis,' said Rennie. 'But he's all right. They're taking him to hospital for an operation.'

A murmur ran around the assembly and chattering broke out. Rennie noticed next, the white ambulance standing on the quay. The driver was edging it nearer to the yacht, and the crowd fell back to make way. As the *Spindrift's* deck was almost level with the quay there would be little difficulty in carrying Brett ashore, Rennie thought thankfully.

Now Craig was back in her view, carrying a stretcher from the ambulance, assisted by a swarthy young man. Andrew had secured the gangplank and the two men came back on board and went below. The children were all agog over what was happening, wanting to run about to see everything, and Rennie had to be very firm with them to keep them well out of range of the activity. Within a minute or two Brett was being carried ashore, with Peta following anxiously behind.

Rennie watched the stretcher lifted into the ambulance. Craig was speaking to Peta, who nodded vigorously, and then they both glanced back at *Spindrift*. Craig suddenly strode swiftly towards the gangway.

Pausing there, he called to Rennie, 'Do you think you could lend a hand? My theatre sister is away and as we don't have a very big staff here, I've no-one very experienced in theatre work.'

Rennie's heart lurched. She had not expected this, and her first thought was that he must believe Brett was seriously ill.

'I...I...' She was momentarily lost for words.

Peta had joined Craig. 'I'll take over the children, Rennie,' she said, adding, 'Do you mind?' Her anxious eyes appealed to Rennie, and Rennie knew she wanted her to assist at the operation. It was a compliment, but it was not just that, it was simple duty which made her say at last, 'Yes, of course I'll assist.'

'You'd better come with us right away,'

Craig said briskly. 'I'll operate at once.'

Rennie, who knew every nuance in his tone was convinced now that he was more anxious about Brett's condition than he was letting on. She felt sure that he was expecting complications. Otherwise why ask her to assist? Surely he must have at least one nurse capable of assisting in the theatre even if his Sister was away.

Rennie felt dazed, like a sleepwalker, moving automatically but only dimly aware of what she was doing, as she handed the children back to Peta, and then accompanied Craig in the ambulance. He did not speak as they drove the short distance from the harbour to the hospital, and Rennie was too painfully conscious of him to notice anything of her surroundings beyond a general impression of hot sunshine and vibrant colour.

Her senses, however, sharpened once they were at the hospital. If she was only half aware of the low white building surrounded by lush green tropical growth, liberally sprinkled with brilliant flowers, she became totally alert once inside and confronted with a familiar routine.

'Nurse Raoul will show you where to scrub up and give you a gown,' Craig said in the same brisk impersonal tone, leaving her finally in the care of the young nurse who had accompanied him to the yacht. He barely looked at her and when he did his expression was unreadable. She might have been any total stranger, fortuitously able to help out in an emergency.

Nurse Raoul showed Rennie the scrub-up room, and provided her with a sterile gown, cap and mask, and shoes. They smiled hesitantly at each other.

Rennie said, 'I didn't expect to find myself assisting at an operation this morning!'

'I didn't realise you were a nurse,' murmured the girl, apologetically, and added, 'we are not a very big hospital. Tavalei is only a small island, but there are a great many out-islands in the group and people come here from all over. We hope to have a bigger staff soon and better facilities, though. Dr Mackenzie has already made many improvements since he's been here.'

Rennie desperately wanted to ask how long Craig had been on Tavalei, but she did not want to reveal that she already knew him, as that might provoke questions she preferred to avoid for the time being.

There was little time, in any case, for conversation, or idle speculation, or even to take in very much of her surroundings. In the operating theatre, a stark white room, smaller than any operating theatre Rennie had ever been in before, Brett Carmichael was almost ready for the operation. Rennie glanced swiftly around her, noting the equipment, formulating in her mind in advance what Craig would expect of her.

He glanced briefly at her, his eyes cool and penetrating above his mask, as he withdrew the anaesthetic needle from the back of Brett's hand.

'We don't have all the sophisticated facilities of a city hospital,' he said, 'and we all have to turn our hands to more than one job.' Without waiting for any comment from her he went on, 'We have to fly serious cases to New Zealand, but we can cope with a number of straight-forward conditions—like appendicitis for instance.' She sensed a faint smile beneath the mask. 'You are of course, quite familiar with the procedure.'

'Of course,' she answered, and turned her attention to the instrument trolley which another nurse had just wheeled up to the operating table. Her eyes flicked over the array of equipment, checking that everything Craig would require was there. She moved it and herself fractionally closer, and steeled her mind to think of one thing only—the operation. She was here to do a job, and not to allow this man whom she had once loved deeply, and now utterly despised, to intrude.

Rennie had had plenty of experience in the theatre. It was perhaps that part of nursing she enjoyed most. There was something especially satisfying about being part of a team that saved lives in this dramatic way—and to Rennie it always was dramatic repairing bodies and making them whole and functional again.

In spite of her resolve, she could not help wondering why Craig had chosen to come here, to this out of the way place on the other side of the world, as far from Whitehouse General as you could get. It astonished her that a man of his calibre, a surgeon in a big teaching hospital in the north of England, would have wanted to take on an inadequately staffed and ill-equipped tiny hospital on a remote Pacific island.

There was no answer she could find, and Craig was as unlikely to give her one as she was to ask him. His voice came to her through her thoughts and, automatically she responded, just as she always had when she had assisted him at operations, in rather different circumstances.

She watched as she had watched so many times before as he made the first sure, quick incision in Brett's abdomen, and could not help the familiar rush of admiration for his calm, his

47

skill, his efficiency, his total commitment whether the operation was short and simple, or difficult and long. And whatever the operation, whatever demands it made on him, he never forgot that it was a human life at stake. He was a man of great compassion, of deep sympathy and understanding, and these were the things that had made her love him, she supposed, and yet...

She heard his sharp intake of breath and tensed, her involuntary thoughts scattering. He did not look at her or speak but she guessed it was the angry inflammation he had revealed that had caused his slight exclamation. She tried to concentrate her mind wholly on what she was doing, obeying his every instruction swiftly and efficiently, but still one half of her was in torment because he was so close, and her mind kept throwing up the past with startling clarity, despite her resolve not to allow it.

The last time she had seen him, she recalled, it had been in circumstances similar to this—but the operation had been for a hole-in-the-heart on a young boy. She remembered it vividly because in a different way her own heart had been involved. They had been as impersonal with each other then as they were now.

It had all been over between them for some weeks, but nothing had been said. At first she had been going to tell him that she knew he was married, that she despised him for deceiving her; she had resolved not to make a sordid scene but to finish their relationship neatly and tidily, like a wound successfully sutured, the thread cut cleanly and finally.

But her courage had deserted her. On the day she was going to tell him he had said he would come round to see her that evening as usual, and she had suddenly panicked and blurted out something about being tired and wanting to go to bed early. Twice after that she had made other excuses not to see him, and when he had tried to ask what was the matter, instead of telling him, she had fled muttering more excuses.

She had been utterly cowardly, she knew, but it had been more than cowardice that had motivated her. She was afraid—afraid of her own weakness. He would explain, of course, probably tell her his wife didn't understand him, and play on her sympathy. He might even laugh at her for being old-fashioned. And she had loved him so much she had been afraid her emotions might win over her common sense.

It had been a relief when a junior doctor had asked her to go out with him. Instead of refusing as she would have done before, she accepted gladly, and by chance Craig had seen them together. He had avoided her rather obviously after that, and in a desperate bid to assuage her misery Rennie had gone out with anyone who asked her. And yet, although she despised him and wished she had never met him, there were also times when she wished she had never seen the woman who knew him.

Mrs Quinn had only been in hospital briefly for a curettage. The morning she was discharged, a Mrs Bates had been admitted to the next bed. She was to have a hysterectomy. Craig, who was to perform that operation, had apparently looked in for a word with Mrs Bates just as Mrs Quinn was leaving. When Rennie had come into the Women's ward later on, Mrs Quinn had gone and it was Mrs Bates who said:

'Oh, Nurse, I'm so glad it's Dr Mackenzie who is going to do my operation. Wasn't it nice of him to come and see me right away? He was so nice and so reassuring. I feel quite all right about it now. He had a chat to that lady who left this morning too. It turned out that they knew each other, although he didn't do her op. She told me afterwards he's got a lovely wife and two sweet children.' She had smiled teasingly as she added, 'What a shame really! I suppose none of you nurses would have minded him being single!'

Rennie's throat had been too dry to answer. She could only try to pull herself together and smile faintly at the joke. For the rest of that day she had walked about in a state of shock, unable to believe what Mrs Bates had said. Married! She had never dreamed that Craig might be married.

But as she thought about it, suddenly a lot of things seemed to make sense. In all the six months she had known him she had never seen him at weekends, even when they were both off duty together. Although she had talked freely about her family, particularly her father who was a doctor in the West Country, he had always been evasive about his. He had briefly mentioned his own father, also a surgeon, now retired and living with Craig's sister in Edinburgh, but that was all. He had always, she realised, abruptly changed the subject whenever it was becoming personal. There could only have been one reason for that. He had been afraid she would suspect the truth.

It had not occurred to her before, but suddenly it did, that he had also been careful to be very discreet about their relationship. They had never attended any hospital functions together, nor frequented any of the places where hospital staff might see them. And she had not talked about her relationship with him simply because she knew how the hospital gossiped. Perhaps, she thought, she was the only one who didn't know he was married.

But it was certainly not common knowledge, she discovered when she casually commented on it to one or two other nurses. They said the same thing. 'I haven't the foggiest whether he's married or not. He's a bit of a dark horse, isn't he? I suppose I've just assumed he must be married since he never makes a pass at anyone! Why don't you ask him?'

But Rennie knew there was no point in asking him. There had therefore been only one course open to her and she had taken it. She had resigned, determined to put as many miles between her and unhappiness as she could. But while she had to endure Whitehouse General for the duration of her notice, she went out with anyone who asked her, and pretended that there was nothing wrong, that having a good time was all she wanted, and whenever she could she flaunted it before Craig, wanting him to think she didn't care for him any more. But the bitterness was deep and even when she had left and set off to see the world, the misery followed her. Time and distance had not effected the cure she had expected and now, ironically, the whole wretched business had caught up with her, almost two years later.

Suddenly she realised that the operation was over. Half her mind and her hands were still working automatically, her reflexes so well trained they could carry on without her knowing it. She was only vaguely aware of the other nurses, and then through the haze of her memories, Craig's voice filtered in fragments:

'...peritonitis...antibiotics...not dangerous... he's very fit...two or three weeks...'

Rennie was jerked back into the present and she forced herself to meet those cool grey disembodied eyes above his surgical mask, as he went on, 'Don't worry, he'll be all right.' His reassuring tone told her that her own eyes had revealed her tension, but he could not know that it was not because of Brett.

She swallowed hard. She could think of nothing to say, about Brett, about anything.

She felt like a zombie as she watched Brett wheeled away to the recovery room. And then she was alone with Craig, facing him without his mask, seeing the same blank expression as before and wondering what was going on in his mind. Did he ever have any pangs of remorse, she wondered? Did he ever regret deceiving her, pretending to be in love with her, leading her on, letting her believe...

He was speaking again. 'You might as well come across to my house for lunch.'

Rennie was startled. She had not expected an invitation. All she wanted to do now was

53

to go back to the yacht, see Peta and reassure her.

'I think I'd better get back to the yacht,' she said, a little ungraciously.

'I'm sure Mrs Carmichael and Mr Barker would join us if I asked them,' he said easily. 'I'll have someone go and bring them up.' He allowed a half smile. 'Come along, out of that gown, and we'll go. It's been quite a morning...and I believe it was quite a night for you too. You must be in need of some rest.'

Rennie had forgotten that she had had no sleep since the night before last, apart from a doze on the deck yesterday afternoon, but strangely she did not feel tired. She knew she would collapse sooner or later, but at the moment she was too shattered by what was happening to feel sleepy. She would have to exist on her nerves for a few more hours. She felt relieved however that Peta and Andy would be joining them for lunch. Craig alone she was not sure she could cope with yet.

His house, she shortly discovered, was only a stone's throw from the hospital, on the edge of the hospital grounds. They walked to it across green lawns edged with brilliantly flowering hibiscus hedges. Between them there was an uneasy silence. Rennie had the feeling that Craig wanted to speak, but was holding back. There were a million things she wanted to say to him, but none that would come out.

At the house, a low white-painted bungalow nestling amid a forest of tropical greenery and surrounded by a wide cool verandah, Rennie met Anna, Craig's Polynesian housekeeper who looked her over with dark appraising eyes and bestowed on her a wide approving smile.

'Welcome, Miss Phillips,' she said in her slow, musical voice. 'Welcome to Tavalei and the doctor's house.'

'I'm sure Miss Phillips would appreciate a shower, Anna,' Craig said in a tone that made Rennie feel she dare not refuse. She certainly felt like one, so she let Anna show her immediately to a big bright bathroom.

The strong jet of the shower made her skin tingle refreshingly, and the big fluffy bath towel Anna had brought her was sheer luxury. Rennie shook out her shirt and slacks and, dressed in them again, felt a whole lot better. She was wondering where to go next when Anna appeared and directed her to the living room where she said she would find the doctor.

Rennie entered, half expecting—and hoping —to find Peta and Andrew already there, but only Craig was in the room, standing by the large windows overlooking the plant-filled verandah. He had changed, and was now wearing white slacks and a dark blue shirt. His hair was damp and she supposed he must have showered too, in some other bathroom.

Vaguely she wondered where his wife was. His eyes met hers and held them for a moment as she entered the room. Then, moving towards her, he said, 'A cold drink would be welcome, I expect?' His voice was perfectly controlled and if he felt any emotion, his tone certainly did not betray it.

'Thank you.' Rennie was still standing, so he said, 'Do please sit down.'

She sat at one end of a large cane settee with soft plump cushions, and her heart was racing in a most disconcerting manner.

He handed her a tall glass chinking with ice. Her fingers closed around the cold glass and she took a sip. 'Thank you, it's delicious.'

He remained standing before her, looking down at her, until she could stand the silence no longer, so she said, 'You were the last person I expected to find as doctor on the island.'

A smile that was hardly a smile at all, and betrayed some bitterness, moved his lips. Moving away from her, he said, 'You vanished from Whitehouse General in a hurry. It was said... that you had eloped...'

She thought she detected an underlying

innuendo in his use of the rather old-fashioned work. She said, laughing a little nervously,'Who on earth would I have eloped with?'

He shrugged, his grey eyes again appraising her. 'You had plenty of choice as I recall.' Now there was a distinct note of censure in his tone and it made her angry. What right had he to criticise her! Just because she had made a point of going out with everyone who asked her during those last painful weeks when she had been working out her notice, when she had been showing him how little she cared...

Her anger subsided. What was the point of getting uptight about it now?

'Well, perhaps you had some other reason,' Craig said, turning to pour himself another drink. 'Since you were about to qualify as a Sister, your sudden departure naturally gave rise to gossip and some speculation.'

It was not that, Rennie knew, which had given rise to gossip. She coloured faintly under his steady gaze which was again directed at her. They both knew what kind of gossip a hasty exit was likely to produce. At the time it had never occurred to her.

'I decided to see the world,' she said, feeling that it sounded lame. She went on to tell him about her sojourns in Australia and New Zealand and Africa and how she had come to meet the Carmichaels, and then, because she was suddenly aware of how defensive she sounded, she stopped abruptly.

He said unsmilingly, 'I believe you. You'd hardly be here now if it wasn't true.'

Rennie said, 'What made you come out here? It's a far cry from Whitehouse, isn't it?'

'It is indeed.' He swirled the liquid in his glass and swallowed a long draught. 'A far cry indeed.'

'But you had a wonderful job, a career...' she objected, unable to understand what had made him give it up.'

'I've got a very satisfying job here,' he said, 'if you don't measure satisfaction in money terms.'

'Well, I suppose it makes a change,' said Rennie, realising that he was not going to explain fully, not to her at any rate. She added, 'I don't suppose you'll stay here forever.'

He tossed back the remainder of his drink, then toyed for a moment with the empty glass. 'Oddly enough,' he said slowly, 'I might. Tavalei has a number of attractions—a marvellous climate, a leisurely way of life, and it presents a challenge...'

'Challenge?' Rennie was intrigued.

He sat on the cane lounger near her, placing his glass on the nearby table. His grey eyes were earnest and Rennie felt that she was almost forgotten as he went on, 'You see, there is a lot to be done here on the medical scene. There is a crying need for a much bigger hospital. We are the main island of a large group of scattered islands as you doubtless know. Not all are inhabited, but some are quite well populated. We are not equipped to deal with every eventuality but we could be...well, with ninety-nine per cent of cases, anyway. It would be a great convenience, perhaps even a lifesaver at times, if we could treat more cases locally. Local people would appreciate it too. They dislike having to go to New Zealand where their relatives can't visit them. They take longer to get well when they are lonely.'

'Yes, I see,' said Rennie. It was typical of Craig that he would be considering people first and wanting to improve things for them, but she still could not imagine him spending his whole life in a place like this, however beautiful. She longed to ask about his wife, who was at this moment still conspicuous by her absence. Surely she was out here with him. Rennie could not bring herself to mention the subject casually.

A highly charged silence followed. Rennie looked away but felt his gaze still on her. Their former relationship stood between them like a wall and yet it could not be mentioned. Suddenly she was remembering the small intimacies, the tendernesses, the many times when her own passions had almost betrayed her—the one now bitterly regretted time they had—and a shudder ran through her. That he could have been so loving, and yet so false. The hurt came rushing back and she remembered how she had wanted to hurt him too, yet knew she couldn't because he hadn't truly loved her, only used her. She was relieved when Anna came into say that the visitors were just getting out of a taxi.

Craig stood up and went to the door. A moment later the children dashed in and ran to Rennie, full of excitement and tumbling over themselves to tell her all they had seen and done that morning. Andrew lounged in after them and Peta followed with Craig who was firmly reassuring her about Brett.

'You'll be able to see him later on this afternoon,' he was saying.

Andrew flopped down beside Rennie. 'Well, Florence Nightingale, how was it? You look a bit tired, but that's hardly surprising.'

'I'm fine,' Rennie said, wishing he had not placed his good hand over her knee, even if only in a purely friendly gesture of solicitation. She noticed Craig watching them.

He handed cold drinks around and there was much lively chatter for some minutes while the whole situation was discussed, from the storm the previous night to Brett's emergency operation that morning. Craig gave no indication to the others that he and Rennie had known each other previously. She guessed he preferred to avoid any embarrassing questions that might arise. She certainly did. There was no mention either of any family of his, so Rennie was left in a state of puzzlement. It seemed quite plain now that his wife and children were not living on Tavalei with him.

Craig suddenly noticed Andrew's hand and remarked on it. Rennie looked at the blood-stained, now rather loose and grubby bandage. She felt instantly guilty for not having attended to it this morning.

Taking it in her hands to examine it, she said concernedly, 'I'm sorry, Andy, I wish you'd reminded me, and I would have changed the dressing for you.' She looked up at Craig. 'I really think it needs a couple of stitches. I'd like you to look at it if you would. It's a nasty gash, quite deep, but not infected. It's in an awkward place to heal.' She drew her finger lightly across the bandaged palm to indicate the direction of the wound.

'It's quite all right,' protested Andrew. 'No

need to fuss.' He grimaced at Craig. 'Rennie is so solicitious...' He treated her to a long affectionate look, which irritated her although it shouldn't have.

She said firmly, 'I think you should let Dr Mackenzie look at it, Andy.'

He shrugged. 'All right.'

'Straight after lunch,' suggested Craig at once. 'You can come across to the Casualty Room and I'll attend to it there.' There was a sound at the door and he turned, 'Ah...lunch is ready, I think.'

His housekeeper came in. 'Yes, you can come now, if you're ready, Doctor.'

They followed Craig into the big airy dining room that overlooked the garden on one side, and which commanded a distant view of the ocean from windows on the opposite side.

'What a delightful home you have, Doctor,' enthused Peta gazing around her. 'Do you live here alone?'

Rennie caught her breath sharply, awaiting his reply.

'Yes,' he said, 'except for my housekeeper, Anna, who looks after me admirably, as I'm sure you'll agree when you have sampled what she calls lunch.'

Rennie waited for Peta to innocently make some remark about what a pity he didn't have a wife, as in her romantic mind she was probably thinking just that, but Peta merely eyed the table and said, 'I see what you mean. It looks more like a banquet!'

Andrew, who was still admiring the view, turned and said to Craig. 'How long have you been here, Dr Mackenzie?'

'About eighteen months,' Craig answered, with a passing glance at Rennie.

So, she thought, he must have left Whitehouse soon after I did.

'You practised in England before?' asked Peta, as she sat down where he indicated. She smiled up at him. 'Or perhaps Scotland!'

'I trained in Scotland,' he answered pleasantly, motioning Andrew and Rennie to their places, 'but I was at Whitehouse General in Broomswich before I came here.' His glance flickered briefly to Renni, almost in warning.

'Were you really?' exclaimed Peta at once. 'Isn't that where you were nursing, Rennie? What a coincidence! Did you know each other?' She did not seem to think it odd that this was the first time it had been mentioned.

'We were...acquainted,' said Craig slowly.

Rennie, who was helping Anna prop the children up on cushions, kept her face averted as she said, 'Whitehouse General is a big hospital.' She was glad he had acknowledged no more than acquaintanceship, but also grateful that he had taken the initiative in bringing their knowing each other into the open. She disliked deceptions of even the most trivial kind, but she would have found it difficult to sound as casual as he had.

'Well, I do think that's extraordinary,' said Peta, 'don't you, Rennie, you and Dr Mackenzie both having been at the same hospital, and now meeting again on the other side of the world!'

'It's a very small world,' said Craig, smiling laconically, and then added, 'If you have no objections perhaps we could be a little less formal and use each other's first names. You are going to be here for a few weeks I'm afraid, and we will probably be seeing quite a bit of each other.' His eyes flickered around the table, resting fractionally longer on Rennie than anyone else. 'My name is Craig,' he said.

'Peta,' said Peta at once, 'and this is Andrew, my brother. Rennie is really Adrienne, but she likes to be called Rennie, don't you? But I expect you know that...' she trailed off, then as an afterthought, she laughingly added, 'Oh, and I nearly forgot, the children are Damien and Emma!'

Craig was smiling pleasantly. He looked at Rennie. 'Do you prefer Rennie?' he asked.

Rennie answered brightly, 'I don't mind,' but cruel fingers of pain were curling around her heart as she remembered that Craig had called her Adrienne, rolling it off his tongue softly and caressingly. She dared not look at him now for fear her emotion would betray her. She was thankful when the subject immediately turned to food as they began to help themselves from the many wooden bowls of fresh crisp salads, meats and tropical delicacies.

The conversation revolved mainly around the Carmichael's voyage, and Rennie, who was contributing only minor remarks, began to feel very sleepy. Once she even nodded off momentarily but quickly jerked awake with a painful neck wrench, and hoped no-one had noticed. A swift glance from Craig, however, told her that her lapse had not escaped his eagle eye, but he did not remark on it.

After lunch he said, 'If you would like to walk back with me to the hospital, Andrew, I'll attend to that hand. He smiled at Peta. 'And I know you're on tenterhooks about your husband, so you might as well look in on him. He might not be fully conscious though.'

Peta's face showed pleasure and relief. 'Thank you,' she said.

Craig suggested tactfully, 'Perhaps you'd better not take the children to see him just yet.

If Rennie doesn't mind staying here…?'

'Of course not.' Rennie stifled a yawn as she spoke.

Andrew put a protective arm around her shoulders. 'You look as whacked as I feel,' he said, 'I'll just get this hand attended to and then we'll all go back to *Spindrift* to catch up on some sleep.'

Craig said to Rennie, 'We won't be very long.' His lips smiled at her but his expression was remote.

Anna came into the living room as the others were leaving. She regarded Rennie with some concern.

'My dear child, you're nearly dead on your feet! I'll look after the little ones and you make yourself comfortable and have a rest.'

'I'm all right, really,' protested Rennie. 'I'll be able to have a good long sleep once we get back to the yacht. No watches for any of us tonight, thank goodness.'

'Well, you might as well relax for a few minutes while they're gone,' insisted Anna, and ignoring any further protests from Rennie, she bustled the children away.

Rennie sat on the couch where she had been sitting before and gazed out of the window at the lush garden through which the sunshine slanted in golden shafts. A bird called high and clear from somewhere nearby, and there was a sudden chorus of cicadas in the treetops. It was so peaceful that in spite of the enormous strain of the past twenty-four hours, she began to feel relaxed. The last sound she heard was the delighted laughter of the children somewhere in the house.

When Rennie woke it was almost dark. There were ribbons of fiery red across the patch of sky visible from where she was lying full length on the couch, and there was a strong scent of frangipani wafting through an open window. She sat up with a guilty start, not realising where she was for a moment, and then glancing around, saw that she was still in Craig Mackenzie's living room. She was about to get up when he strolled into the room, and seeing she was awake, stopped abruptly.

'Ah...you're awake. I'm afraid I was going to have to waken you if you hadn't been,' he said, coming nearer, and standing looking down at her. It must have been the gloom and her slight sense of disorientation, but he looked taller and broader than usual, and his features seemed more sharply defined, and quite forbidding.

'I...I must have fallen asleep,' she muttered, embarrassed both by what she had done and by his proximity. 'Where are the others?'

'They went back to the yacht and...'

'Why didn't you wake me?' Rennie jumped up, dismayed.

'You looked so peacefully dead to the world, I suggested we didn't disturb you, especially as...'

Again she did not let him finish. 'I'm sorry,' she broke in. 'I'm being a nuisance.'

'Not at all.' His hand touched her arm, and the touch burned her skin as the memory of his hands on her body seared her mind. She felt herself go rigid. He seemed to sense it, and released her abruptly.

'I didn't get any sleep at all last night,' she said.

He nodded. 'I know. I heard all about it from Andrew, who is full of admiration for your seamanship.' There was a hint of mockery in his tone. 'You obviously have talents I never suspected.'

'I don't want to inconvenience you,' Rennie said, 'so perhaps you would telephone for a taxi for me.'

'There's no need,' he said, 'you're staying here.'

Rennie's mouth dropped open. 'Staying here?'

'Yes. Peta and Andrew spoke about moving ashore to sleep as you're going to be here for some time, but accommodation is rather limited on Tavalei, and I know the hotel is fully booked out at the moment. There is a convention here which has rather strained the island's resources, and in a couple of weeks we'll be having our annual Regatta. So I suggested you all stay here. There is plenty of room.'

'But we can't do that...' blurted Rennie, horrified at the thought of living in his house, seeing him every day.

He continued to smile at her in a rather infuriating way. 'Why not? You will not have to endure my company if you do not wish...'

It was as though he had read her mind. 'Don't be silly,' she said, 'it isn't that, it's just that...'

'You feel it's an imposition.'

'Exactly. I'm surprised Peta...'

'She protested very prettily too,' he said, 'but there is no need for any of you to feel obligated. I am delighted to have the opportunity to entertain compatriots—and especially an ex-colleague.' He put a certain emphasis on the last word.

Rennie had the feeling that he was enjoying her discomfort, that this was his way of repaying her for dumping him. Well, he had a nerve! What about the way he had treated her? She bit back further protests however, since if Peta and Andrew had agreed to the arrangement it was scarcely up to her to object. Obviously, for Peta it was ideal to be within a stone's throw of Brett.

'It's very kind of you,' Rennie said quickly, 'very hospitable. I'm sure we are all very grateful.'

He walked towards the door. 'Anna has tonight off,' he told her, 'so we shall be going out to dinner. Now, shall I show you to your room? The others are probably still asleep, but I promised to wake them in time for dinner.'

As they went out onto the verandah, Rennie said, 'I'll rouse Peta if you like and you can wake Andy.'

He glanced down at her. 'Oh, I thought you would prefer it the other way around.'

Rennie reacted sharply to his acid tone. 'I don't see why.'

He shrugged and did not answer, but Rennie guessed that he had assumed a relationship between her and Andy. Well, what did it matter if he had?

They walked along to the end of the verandah and he pointed out Peta and the children's rooms, and her own.

'Andrew is in the bungalow in the garden,' he said, pointing to a thatched roof just visible between a thicket of banana palms.

Rennie said again, 'It's very generous of you to have us...'

'Not at all. I shall enjoy it immensely.' He flung open her door. 'If you need anything, give me a call, and if I can't supply it, Anna will see to it in the morning. Andrew brought your gear up from the yacht so I expect you'll find everything you want.'

'Thank you,' Rennie murmured yet again.

He did not go. The dusk was deepening now and cicadas were singing lustily in all corners of the garden. The scent of frangipani was strong, and other perfumes were mingled with it in a heady fragrance. Rennie saw a star twinkle above a palm tree silhouetted against the sky and suddenly her heart was racing again as Craig continued to stand there, looking at her. That he should still have the power to stir her emotions after the way he had treated her, angered her.

She said sharply, 'Well, I'd better call Peta, I suppose, and then get showered and changed.' She turned a little too quickly, as he too turned away from her door to cross the lawn to the bungalow, and they almost walked into each other's arms.

Rennie began hastily to step aside but found herself firmly clasped and drawn so swiftly back towards him she had no time to resist. His arms tightened around her and she could feel her heart thumping madly against her ribcage. For an interminable moment their eyes locked, each scarcely able to see the other's face in the gloom, with something so strong between them that Rennie could only remain rigidly a prisoner of his encircling arms.

When he bent his head and kissed her, long and hungrily, and softly murmured her name, 'Adrienne...' just as he had always done, she was for a moment totally lost, drowned in the marvel of being in his arms, his warm breath on her neck, her cheeks, and all the hostility she felt for him was overridden, and she loved him as she had before, without reservation, until sharply the reminder came. He was married. He had deceived her once, letting her believe he loved her, and he would do so again. He had taken all she had to give, knowing he would give nothing back. He had used her, and she was not going to let that happen again. She was not going to love him.

She wrenched free of him. 'Don't touch me!' she said, through clenched teeth, her voice low, and furious. 'It's over, Craig, over—and I don't want to start anything again.'

Momentarily a spark of something close to anger showed in his face. His eyes narrowed, and a nerve near the corner of his mouth twitched. Then abruptly he drew away from her, saying softly, 'Sorry, I should have had more control. It won't happen again.'

He swung his strong athletic body round and shoulders squared, walked across the lawn towards the bungalow, disappearing in a moment into the banana palms. Rennie, choking on a sob that rose from deep inside her, watched him disappear and then with a feeling like the heartbreak she had known two years ago when she had reluctantly broken with him, she went into her own room, unable to face Peta for a minute or two.

CHAPTER THREE

'He's rather dishy, isn't he?' Peta remarked as she and Rennie strolled along the verandah presently, to join the men prior to going out to dinner.

'Who?' murmured Rennie absently, her mind still numbed by her earlier encounter with Craig. Her own response to him still appalled her. It would be so easy she had discovered, to slide back into their old relationship, which evidently he was not averse to doing, even for the short time she would be here.

She hated him for it, and yet he drew her like a magnet, like no other man had ever done. The worst of it was that being in his arms again had forced her to acknowledge that many times she had regretted breaking with him, that running away had really been to stop herself returning to him—on his terms. The knowledge disgusted her. How could she let a man who had treated her as he had, insinuate himself into her whole being like some deadly incurable disease? She felt ashamed all over again, and involuntarily shuddered.

Peta exclaimed laughingly, 'Craig, of course! He's gorgeous! I bet all the nurses at Whitehouse were crazy about him. Maybe that's what he's really doing here—running away from them!' Her laughter rippled out across the dusky starlit garden.

Rennie brushed away a moth that fluttered around her head as they passed under one of the verandah lights. She was tempted to say, 'he's married,' but bit back the words. It was not up to her to reveal it. Where was his wife, she wondered, yet again? She burned with curiosity but knew she would never dare ask. And what about his children? Where were they now?

Peta paused to pick a frangipani flower. She held it to her noise, breathing in its perfume. 'What's the matter, Rennie? Are you feeling all right?'

Rennie was well aware that she was behaving rather oddly. 'Oh, yes, I'm fine,' she said quickly. 'Sorry...I was drifting there for a moment. What was it you said?'

Peta looked at her quizzically. 'I was wondering if the handsome doctor was on the run from the nurses at Whitehouse!'

Rennie forced a light response. 'He might well be! He was very popular as I recall.' It was

75

more likely, she thought, that he had run away from his wife and family.

'But not with you?' Rennie realised that Peta was repeating the question and her candid hazel eyes were searching Rennie's altogether too shrewdly.

Rennie walked on slowly. 'I didn't know him well.' This in one way was true. She had thought she had known him, every part of him, and she had been wrong. He had been deceiving her all the time.

Peta shrugged and dropped the subject, to Rennie's relief. She said, 'Isn't this a heavenly place, Rennie? It's really very generous of Craig to let us stay in his house. I protested like mad, but he was adamant. It'll be a nice change from the yacht for a while.' She slid a smile across to Rennie. 'Actually, I think he's probably rather lonely and a bit homesick, and that's why he jumped at the chance of having fellow countrymen to stay, especially a former nurse from Whitehouse. He'll be able to gossip with you to his heart's content.'

'I shouldn't think he has much time for gossiping,' said Rennie. 'I get the impression the life of a doctor on Tavalei is a very busy one.'

They walked through the vestibule towards the living room. Rennie caught a glimpse of herself in a long cane-framed mirror. She was a shade taller than Peta and a shade slimmer. Seeing herself in the pale mint green cotton dress that was low-necked and sleeveless, and flared becomingly from a high waistline, she was surprised to find that she looked quite cool and relaxed. She wore no jewellery and her make-up was minimal. Her bright blonde hair clung fetchingly about her face, the ends flicked up against her cheeks. As she passed close to the mirror she saw that her eyes looked wider and greener than usual, reflecting the colour of her dress and thin strappy sandals.

The men were waiting in the living room. Both were wearing white trousers and blue reefer jackets, but Andrew had on a very pale pink shirt and paisley cravat, while Craig sported a light blue roll-neck skivvy. Rennie felt both pairs of eyes on her as they entered, Andrew's smiling and admiring, openly flirtatious, while Craig's gaze was dark and brooding and his smile seemed forced. She guessed that now he was wishing he had not invited them to stay in his house. Both men rose to greet the girls, and Craig said, 'A drink before we go?' He crossed the room to a bamboo cocktail bar. 'Peta, what would you like? Rennie?'

Peta considered briefly. 'I'd love a gin and lime. Do you have it?'

'Most certainly,' he replied, and as he took a glass from the rack above the bar, glanced again at Rennie. 'Rennie?'

'Oh...yes, I'd like that too,' she answered hurriedly, aware that her mind had moment-arily drifted again as it always seemed to be doing these past few hours. She really must pull herself together.

Andrew came to her side. 'Come and sit down. How are you feeling now?'

She should have been touched and flattered by his concern, but for some reason she felt ir-ritated by him. She replied rather shortly, 'I'm fine. I feel so bad dropping off to sleep like that.'

Andrew laughed. 'It was a wonder you didn't drop over lunch.' His eyes roved slowly over her face, straying down to where her dress revealed the firm smooth contours of her breasts. 'You look lovely now, all fresh and cool...'

'As an iced gin and lime...' There was an edge to Craig's voice even though he smiled as he handed Rennie her glass, chinking with ice, a curl of fresh lime floating between the cubes.

She took it without looking at him, and Andrew laughed. He placed a hand along her thigh as he said, 'But not so frosty, though!'

Rennie wanted to slap his hand away, to fly

78

at him for being so unnecessarily suggestive, but she bit back the sudden rush of annoyance. It was Andrew's injured hand that lay on her knee.

'How's the hand?' she asked.

'Sewn up like a rent sail!' he answered. 'Craig suggests we carry sutures in future. He says you know how to stitch in time...'

Rennie caught a rather arch look from Craig, and said nothing. They talked for a few minutes while they finished their drinks and then all set off for the hospital to see Brett briefly before continuing on to dinner at the Tavalei Hotel. It seemed natural as they left the house for Craig to walk with Peta, Andrew with Rennie.

Andrew linked Rennie's arm through his. 'Quite an idyllic spot,' he remarked. 'Maybe I'll quit boat-building and become a beach-comber.'

'You'd soon get bored,' Rennie replied, try-ing not to let her eyes concentrate on the tall, broad-shouldered figure that walked just ahead of them up the path, walking with that familiar slow, measured gait, his head tilted down to catch what Peta was saying, his arms swinging loosely at his sides, and his hair flopping slight-ly across his forehead.

If only she could treat him as someone she had just met. But that was impossible. The weeks they might have to stay on Tavalei, she knew, were going to be torture. Unless, she glanced at Andrew, unless she deliberately focussed all her attention on Andy. He wouldn't object, and perhaps he just might keep her mind off Craig.

Brett was awake but still groggy. Nevertheless he greeted them with a tentative smile and an attempt at heartiness.

'Ho, there, shipmates!'

'How are you, Brett?' It was the first time Rennie had seen him since the operating table.

'Pulling through, so the delightful young nurse who satifies my every whim assures me!' he said, with a mischievous grin at his wife.

'That sounds like you,' she rejoined, holding his hand tightly, and looking happier than Rennie had seen her for twenty-four hours. 'Playing at Don Juan the minute I'm out of the way!'

He glanced at Craig, a glint in his eyes. 'Well, seeing you're getting off with the handsome doctor, I have to console myself somehow! Where are you off to now?'

'Craig is taking us to dinner at the Tavalei Hotel,' said Peta.

'Half your luck!'

Craig said, 'You must excuse me for a few minutes. I want to check one or two things with the night staff, and let them know where I'll be. I'll see you outside the main door shortly. Don't tire the patient, will you?' He looked for confirmation to Rennie. 'Only a few minutes tonight, I think.'

She nodded, and whispered to Andrew as Craig strode out, 'Come on, let's leave them alone, shall we?'

Andrew agreed softly, and then aloud he said, 'We'll wait outside, Peta. Take care, Brett. See you later.'

Peta gave them a grateful smile.

As Rennie and Andrew emerged from the cool air-conditioned interior of the hospital, the humid night wrapped itself around them like a warm blanket, and the faint clinging smells of disinfectant and floor polish were quickly superseded by the perfumes of the night. They stood on the verandah of the hospital, near the steps, looking down into the lush tropical garden. Hibiscus bushes flanked the steps, one with brilliant crimson stamens, the other with pure white flowers with red and yellow stamens. The blooms were still open under the verandah lights. Moths and other insects began to buzz around then so Andrew drew Rennie down the steps away from the light. As they passed the white hibiscus, he plucked a bloom and then, drawing her close to him, placed it solemnly in the groove between her breasts.

He kissed her lightly on the forehead, saying softly, 'Don't tell me warm tropical nights, frangipani scented, don't make you feel romantic?'

'Oh, a bit, I suppose,' she answered teasingly, 'but remember what we agreed?'

His eyes met hers. 'I've got a shocking memory! But I promise I won't ever do anything you don't want me to. And you can't deny you like to kiss because I know different...' His lips hovered near hers tantalisingly.

'You'll smudge my lipstick,' Rennie murmured.

His mouth was very close to hers. He placed his hand in the small of her back and exerted enough pressure to draw her even closer to him. 'You'd drive a man wild, wouldn't you?' he murmured with some fervour.

'Peta still with Brett?' Craig's voice came from the top of the steps, and Rennie started back guiltily as though she had been caught out breaking some hospital rule.

'No, I'm right here.' Peta appeared behind him, and they came down the steps together, Craig's hand under her elbow as she was saying how pleased she was to find Brett so perky. Her eyes were sparkling and Rennie felt glad.

She understood Peta's agony this morning. She loved her Brett so very, very much.

As they walked towards Craig's car which was parked just inside the hospital gates in the car park, Andrew and Rennie were a few paces behind the other two. He remarked in a low voice, 'I think Dr Mackenzie rather fancies our Peta.'

Rennie gave a start. She had not considered it, but Andrew's remark made her suddenly fearful, and angry too. Surely Craig would not try to take advantage of Brett's illness—or would he? He had failed with her, and he had few scruples, it seemed, when it came to physical desires. Peta was a very attractive woman. Rennie immediately felt all her hostility towards him boiling up.

Andrew was laughing softly. 'He won't get far with Peta, though. One false move and she'll floor him with a karate chop.'

'Karate?' whispered Rennie, astonished.

'Didn't you know? She's a brown belt. There was this guy in Sydney who tried it on with her one night at a party we went to, and she laid him out cold!'

Rennie almost burst out laughing. It would be a lesson to Craig if Peta did that to him. He was so convinced of his irresistibility to women, so smug and cocksure. She almost hoped he would make a pass at Peta just so that she could put him in his place.

The Tavalei Hotel was a single story building built in island style. There was a large open-sided dining area under a thatched roof, around which palm frond torches flickered. The smoke gave off an aromatic perfume. A local band was playing well-known popular tunes, but with an underlying rhythm characteristic of Polynesian music. A few people were dancing languidly on the central dance floor, others were already eating.

Craig's party was led to a table near the edge of the garden, where a fountain splashed into a small pond and goldfish swam about, and the lush surrounding plants were lit from beneath by concealed lighting.

A bowl of half-closed hibiscus flowers decorated the centre of the table, and a candle glowed in a hollowed-out coconut shell. Escorted by a white-clad waiter who seemed to know Craig well, and treated him very deferentially, they sat down, Rennie and Andrew on one side of the table, Craig and Peta on the other.

Rennie was opposite Craig. Her eyes met his before she could avoid it and then his drifted slowly and embarrassingly down over her face and neck, and he said with a faintly ironic

84

smile, 'Your flower will unfortunately wilt in so warm a place. Perhaps it would be better to put it with the others in the bowl.'

Rennie had by this time forgotten about the hibiscus bloom Andrew had picked. She coloured faintly at the reminder, but could hardly do otherwise than he suggested, even though removing the flower, she realised, gave him an unrestricted view of her cleavage which he clearly intended to enjoy. She wished now she had worn a less revealing dress, and throughout the meal, every time she bent forward to raise a forkful of food to her mouth, she was conscious of Craig's eyes upon her.

She was also conscious after a short time that a beautiful dark-haired girl who had arrived with a small party shortly after them, was constantly turning her head in their direction. Eventually she came over to their table.

'Good evening, Craig,' she murmured, standing next to him, and resting a hand on his shoulder.

He looked up at her and smiled. 'Oh, hello, Lilianne.' He introduced Peta, Andrew and Rennie, explaining about the yacht and Brett's illness.

'I did hear there was some fuss and bother this morning,' said Lilianne in a dismissive tone, as though it was a matter much too trivial for her attention. She smiled at each of them politely but her interest, Rennie saw at once, was in Craig alone.

Craig said, 'Lilianne's father, Alan Henderson, owns this hotel, and his company is also the main exporter of produce from the islands.' He glanced around in the direction from which she had appeared, then said to the girl, 'Inspection night, is it?'

She laughed gaily, and her long fingers tipped with well-manicured scarlet nails moved lightly on Craig's shoulder, suggesting a familiarity between them more than just acquaintance. Rennie wondered just how close they were.

'Yes,' Lilianne said. 'Daddy likes to take them by surprise so he can see exactly what sort of service the paying customers are getting. Why don't you come and join us, Craig? Daddy and Theo are being rather boring talking business, and Mother loves hearing about adventures.' She smiled winningly at the rest of the party, but Rennie felt her eagerness was primarily a ploy to get Craig to her table.

Craig glanced questioningly around. 'All right with you?'

It was clear that he did not want to refuse so they agreed, although Rennie felt sure that Peta, like her, would rather not have mingled with strangers tonight.

Waiters were summoned and the tables re-arranged to accommodate the larger party, while Craig introduced Peta, Andrew and Rennie to the Andersons. Mr Anderson was a rather bluff Yorkshireman, and his wife appeared to be part Polynesian. Looking again at Lilianne, Rennie realised from whom she had inherited her slightly slanting eyes, prominent cheek bones, and the full lips that gave her a striking kind of beauty. She had the long-limbed languorous bearing of an islander too, which in her became a casual elegance. Rennie suspected she had probably been educated abroad and had somwhere acquired a veneer of sophistication. It was no accident, Rennie decided, that Craig sat next to her. For the rest of the evening she monopolised his attention very successfully.

Rennie danced with Andrew a couple of times, and once with Theo Anderson, a cheerful young man, but rather shy. She found his company hardly diverting enough to keep her eyes from straying to Craig and his companion. Eventually Craig asked her to dance, but she refused, saying she felt tired.

'Of course you must be, despite your rest this afternoon,' Craig said solicitiously. 'I think it's time we broke up the party.'

'Oh, no, don't do that just for me,' she protested.

Andrew, who had heard the exchange, said, 'I'm rather tired myself. I'll walk Rennie back. It's not far and I think I can remember the way.'

Peta was quick to add, 'I'm about ready to drop too. I'll come with you. There's no need for you to drive us, Craig. It's a beautiful night for a stroll.'

Lilianne looked delighted at the suggestion that the three were leaving, no doubt anticipating having Craig entirely to herself for the rest of the evening. However, Craig rose, saying, 'As a matter of fact, I'm feeling rather tired too. I was up until all hours last night with a difficult breach birth, so I could do with an earlier night tonight. With this convention in town there are bound to be a few extra minor ailments and accidents wanting attention in the morning.'

Lilianne pouted. 'Oh, Craig, stay a little longer. It's not all that late...'

Craig shook his head. 'Not tonight, Lilianne.'

Mrs Anderson rose and said, 'I think it's time we retired anyway, Alan. You've got those people from Australia arriving tomorrow, don't forget.'

He got up and nodded agreement. A rather petulant expression hardened Lilianne's face, and Rennie decided that she was spoilt and too used to getting her own way.

'I'm sorry, Craig,' Peta said, as they were getting into his car. 'We didn't mean to drag you away.'

'You didn't,' he said. 'I'm sorry for inflicting the Andersons on you when you would probably rather have had a quiet evening, but I didn't want to spurn their hospitality.' He added quietly, 'Alan Anderson is a very generous benefactor of the hospital. He is going to finance some quite big additions and improvements. It's to his advantage of course, as his ultimate aim is to expand tourism on Tavalei.'

Back at the hospital Craig left them to continue on to the house alone. Peta said a brief goodnight to Rennie and Andrew and disappeared into her room. She had purposely given them the opportunity to be alone, Rennie knew, wishing she had not.

When Andrew drew her into his arms, she said stiffly, 'I really am very tired, Andy.'

'Just one kiss,' he said.

Rennie remembered her earlier thought that Andrew might stop her thinking about Craig, so she raised her lips to his and let him kiss her, but there was no fire in their contact, no stirring of her deepest feelings the way there had been when Craig had kissed her. But perhaps it would come in time.

She drew away. 'Goodnight, Andy.'

He smiled down at her confidently. 'Goodnight, Rennie.'

At least, she thought, he wasn't going to rush her. He strode off towards the bungalow and at the same moment there was the sound of footsteps on the wooden verandah. Rennie turned and saw Craig approaching. Her heart began to hammer. Her fingers gripped the handle of her bedroom door as she said, 'Goodnight, Craig,' as he came level with her.

He stopped, looked down at her searchingly, and she knew he had seen her kissing Andrew. 'Goodnight, Rennie,' he said tersely, and walked swiftly on towards his own room at the other end of the house.

The next morning Rennie woke to find sunlight streaming into the room as Anna drew the curtains. Beside the bed was a tray loaded with fruit, coffee, bacon and eggs, and fresh bread. Rennie sniffed the mix of appetising aromas hungrily as she sat up.

Anna beamed at her. 'You slept well?' She answered her own question. 'I can see that you did. You look much better this morning, fully rested now. Eat up your breakfast—you need fattening up, and the other one too. Much too thin!'

Rennie laughed. Against the considerable bulk of the smiling Anna, both she and Peta were bean poles. 'This smells delicious,' she said, reaching for the coffee pot, 'but you shouldn't be spoiling us by giving us breakfast in bed.'

Anne shrugged. 'Doctor Mac said you must be left to rest for as long as you wanted.' She came over to the bed. 'He also said that when you were up, would you go up to the hospital. He would like to talk to you.'

'About Brett, I suppose,' murmured Rennie absently.

'He didn't say,' replied Anna.

Suddenly Rennie felt apprehensive. Supposing he wanted to talk about their former relationship? No, he wouldn't want to do that. It was over long ago, and she had made it quite clear only yesterday, when he had forgotten himself for a moment, that it could not be revived.

When Anna had gone she spent a leisurely half hour eating her breakfast, then another having a shower and getting dressed. Anna, she discovered, had hung all her clothes in the wardrobe, and she must have pressed her few dresses as they were all without a crease. She must remember to thank her.

As soon as she was dressed, today in a blue and white striped button-through dress and white sandals, Rennie went to Peta's room and knocked. She had heard the sounds of the children squealing through the walls, so guessed Peta was awake. She found her still in her nightdress, playing with Damien and Emma.

'Rennie! I hope we didn't wake you?'

'No, Anna did an hour ago. I've had breakfast. I suppose you have too.'

Peta nodded, and patted her firm flat stomach. 'I'm going to put on weight, I can tell. But the food is gorgeous, isn't it? How are you this morning?'

'Fine. One good night's sleep and I'm as right as rain. Now, shall I take the kids off your hands while you shower and dress?'

'All right. You can have them for a bit.' Peta grinned, languishing on the bed, her hands clasped behind her head. 'This is the life! I can stand being pampered, and Craig seems determined that we shall be. I feel quite guilty about it though.'

'He wouldn't do it if he didn't want to,' remarked Rennie.

'No, I suppose not. We were lucky to find such a hospitable doctor.' Her face clouded briefly. 'He has told me the truth about Brett, hasn't he?'

'Yes, of course,' Rennie reassured her at once. 'There's nothing to worry about, Peta. There's some infection which may take a little while to clear up, but you can rely on Craig. He'll look after Brett.'

'He's a good surgeon?'

'One of the best,' confirmed Rennie emphatically.

Peta looked reassured but Rennie suspected that she would continue to worry about Brett until he was out of bed and walking around again. She gathered up the children in her arms and staggered outside with them, to engage in fairly energetic games on the lawn while their mother was in the bathroom. Then she washed and dressed them and gave them back to Peta.

'Craig wants a word with me up at the hospital,' she said casually.

'Oh, yes,' said Peta vaguely. 'He did mention it...'

'Mention what?' Rennie said sharply.

'You run along and have a chat to him,' said Peta, 'I'll take the kids for a walk, I think.'

Rennie was a shade puzzled, but it was obvious Peta would not be drawn. She would rather not have gone up to the hospital as Craig had requested. She still felt uneasy. Probably all he wanted to talk about was Brett, and she was being silly. Nevertheless she determined, as she walked up the hibiscus-lined path, she would refuse to discuss the past if he brought it up. She just wanted to forget all that.

She did not know where Craig's office was, so she by-passed the side entrance they had used last night, and went around to the front of the building, knowing she would find someone there to direct her. It was a shock when she entered to see that the girl at the reception desk, in starched white cap and pale blue uniform with white trim, was Lilianne Anderson. No-one had mentioned that she was a nurse, last night, or if they had, Rennie had somehow missed it.

'Good morning,' Rennie said, 'I had no idea you were a nurse, Lilianne.'

Lilianne eyed her rather coolly. 'Good morning.' Her long dark hair was coiled up into a French roll at the back of her head. Her nurse's cap was perched at a jaunty angle. She looked younger than she had last night in more sophisticated attire. Her nails were no longer scarlet and gone was the iridescent eye-shadow. Her dark, well-shaped brows needed no extra colouring, and her full sensuous lips flaunted this morning only the palest of pink lipstick.

Ignoring Rennie's remark, she added airily,

'Did you want something?'

'Craig said he wanted to see me,' Rennie answered. She noticed the lines between the girl's brows deepen, as she swept Rennie with a speculative gaze. She was obviously curious to know why, but since Rennie did not know herself, she could not enlighten her.

Lilianne came out from behind the desk. 'Come this way,' she said, in a tone that was less than friendly.

Rennie followed her down a corridor to a door inscribed Dr Mackenzie. She knocked and the familiar voice bade them enter. Rennie walked into his office behind Lilianne, feeling rather as though she had been called in to be hauled over the coals for some misdemeanour. Her nervousness mounted as he looked sternly at her from behind his desk.

He rose. 'Thank you, Lilianne.' His tone was crisply dismissive, and Lilianne, who had been inclined to linger, Rennie thought, withdrew reluctantly. Craig continued to look at Rennie without speaking until the door had clicked shut. It was a disconcerting gaze. Finally he said, 'Thank you for coming.'

'What did you wish to see me about?' she asked, anxious to have the interview over and done with. 'Is it about Brett? There are no further complications...?'

He was shaking his head. 'No. He's not out of the wood yet, and we'll have to keep a careful eye on him, but at the moment the prognosis is excellent. He's got a good strong constitution.' He paused, then said, 'Please sit down, Rennie.' He indicated the cane chair near where she was standing.

She sat down since it seemed idiotic to insist on remaining standing, and waited for him to speak again. He seemed more intent however on studying her face. At last he too sat down again. Linking his fingers together, elbows on the desk, and leaning forward slightly, he surprised her by saying, 'I'm going to ask a favour of you.'

'A favour?' Rennie was startled.

He went straight on, 'Brett is a very fit man and will certainly recover quite quickly from the operation, if no further complications occur, which I do not anticipate, but as there is a lot of ocean before your next landfall, I feel that a little longer than usual convalescence would be wise. I talked to Peta about it last night, without being too arbitrary of course, as it will depend largely on Brett's progress, and she has agreed to persuade him to be sensible.'

'I don't see what that has to do with me...' began Rennie.

He smiled, the slow smile that had once

melted her heart every time she encountered him. 'I believe I told you that the only Sister on the staff is in New Zeland at the moment,' he went on, 'convalescing after a rather serious operation for gall stones. She won't be back for another three or four weeks, so I was wondering if you would consider assisting at the hospital while you are stranded here? It would relieve a great burden and perhaps save some cases having to be flown out. I do not have anyone with your experience. My other nurses are all very young and inexperienced and need someone to guide them. I can't be around all the time.'

Rennie was stunned. It was a proposition she could never have imagined, and her first inclination was to refuse. The last thing she wanted was to work in close proximity to him. Living in his house was bad enough. Yet, how could she not agree? He was being more than generous by allowing them to live in his house, and Peta had told her that he had refused quite definitely any recompense. This was one way she could help repay their debt to him.

'You should really ask Peta,' she said. 'I am employed by her to look after the children.'

Her feeling that he had already discussed it with Peta was borne out when he said, 'I know. Peta is perfectly agreeable to the arrangement, if you are. I have offered her the services of my housekeeper in exchange for you. Anna adores children and she will look after them as well as anyone. So, it's up to you, Rennie.'

Rennie bit her lip. She had no alternative but to agree to do what he wanted.

She said, 'Of course, I'll be glad to help.'

His unwavering gaze met hers and she wished she knew what he was thinking at that moment. Did he really need her help, or was this a deliberate plan to disconcert her, to punish her first for dumping him in England, then for rebuffing his advance last night. She realised suddenly that although she might not have hurt his heart, she had undoubtedly dented his pride.

He said slowly, 'Of course, if you feel it's too much of an imposition, you must say so.'

'Not at all. Obviously I am going to have quite a bit of time on my hands, so it will give me something to do.'

He was silent for a moment. 'I am very grateful, Rennie. Sister Donaldson will be back in a few weeks and your filling the breach will save us having to fly out a temporary replacement, which the agency in Wellington has so far been unable to find.'

'When would you like me to start?' Rennie asked resignedly.

'As soon as you can.'

She rose abruptly. 'Then it might as well be right away. If someone would like to find me a uniform and you'd ask someone to show me around...' She made her words brisk and businesslike. She was anxious to be out of his presence as soon as possible.

'I'll take you round myself, and familiarise you with our routine,' Craig said, rising too, and coming to her side of the desk. 'We are a little less formal you'll find than at Whitehouse General!' He smiled, regarding her steadily for a moment, then he said again, 'Thank you, Rennie. I'm immensely grateful.'

Momentarily, she experienced a rush of emotion that almost overwhelmed her and pushed her into his arms. It was only with a super-human effort that she managed to prevent such a catastrophe. She was only going to be here for a few weeks, and any rekindling of old fires would be foolish in the extreme. She would be no more to him now than she had been before.

CHAPTER FOUR

Rennie's first days at Tavalei Hospital proved to be busy ones. Although there were only about a dozen patients to look after, requiring simple routine nursing which the other nurses attended to mostly, with so many visitors on the island for the convention, there was the inevitable rash of minor accidents and illnesses.

Rennie found herself occupied for much of her time assisting Craig at his morning Surgery, helping in the Casualty Room when required, dealing with the routines of the Pre-natal Clinic and the Infant Welfare Clinic. And all the time, as she cleaned and dressed an assortment of cuts and abrasions, soothed babies and small children, administered medicines and gave injections, she was painfullly aware of Craig's presence. All the time she was conscious of the suppressed hostility between them, which occasionally erupted in a sharp word of criticism from him when she had done something not quite to his liking, or a terseness on her part when she was obliged to ask him something.

Much of what she was doing, she realised again and again, could have been done just as competently by any of the other nurses, but Craig seemed determined to keep her at his right hand as much as possible, which she suspected was deliberately to make her feel uncomfortable. He had said at first when he had told her she would be staying in his house that she need not see much of him if she didn't want to, now he was ensuring that she did.

One person who deeply resented this was Lilianne Anderson, and she did not trouble to conceal her dislike of Rennie. She spoke to her only when necessary, and if Rennie felt obliged to direct her in some small duty, she would toss her dark head superciliously and be as unco-operative as she could. Even after the first day, Rennie was wishing she did not have to go through with it, but there was no backing out now. When Lilianne did unbend sufficiently to speak casually to Rennie, it was invariably to mention Craig in connection with herself, how he had escorted her on this or that occasion, how highly her parents regarded him, and underlying her remarks was always the suggestion of a special relationship. Rennie often wondered if Lilianne knew Craig was married with two children.

There was one bright spot in Rennie's hospital duties and that was Nurse Raoul, whom Rennie had taken to at once. She was always friendly and helpful to her, and eager to co-operate and, like the other nurses apart from Lilianne, did not seem to resent her, but was grateful for her wider experience and help.

Jeanette Raoul was a placid, sweet-tempered girl who never seemed to get flustered about anything, even Lilianne, when that girl was flouncing about as she so often did. The patients all loved her and after a few days of watching her approach to nursing, Rennie decided it was no wonder. The girl had more than just natural ability, she had a spontaneous good nature and deep compassion, but more than that, she had a magic touch. The contrast with Lilianne was sharp. Lilianne was, Rennie feared, barely average as a nurse, and she often wondered how long the girl would stick at it.

'So long as she thinks she's got a chance with Dr Mackenzie,' said Jeanette with a wry smile one morning.

She and Rennie were having a cup of morning coffee in the nurses's room over-looking the garden, and having just come from a particularly exasperating encounter with Lilianne, Rennie had given vent to her feelings, although aware she should not have done.

'I thought it might be something like that,' she said.

Jeanette went on kindly, 'It's a shame really. Lilianne is not cut out for nursing. She's intelligent, but far too impatient. She is only doing it because her parents insisted she train for something, and it was a chance to get away from Tavalei for a while. She doesn't really like nursing. She'll be happier when she's married.'

'Do you think she'll marry Dr Mackenzie?' Rennie could not help asking.

Jeanette shrugged. 'Lilianne is the kind of girl who always get what she wants.' She smiled. 'Perhaps I'm being unfair. Dr Mackenzie has a mind of his own and I'm sure he would not marry her unless he really wanted to.'

Or was able to, thought Rennie. The thought struck her then that perhaps he was now divorced; it was possible in the time. But more likely, she believed, was that he was just stringing Lilianne along as he had her.

Feeling she ought not to continue discussing Lilianne, Rennie asked, 'How long have you been nursing, Jeanette?'

Jeanette stirred her coffee and took a biscuit from the tin with long delicate fingers. 'Nearly two years.'

'You love it, don't you?'

The girl nodded. 'But I don't want to spend

103

all my life here. I want to travel and broaden my experience by working in other places—in big hospitals overseas.' She sighed. 'Some time perhaps I will go to New Zealand or Australia, even Europe, who knows!' She laughed at herself. 'I'm too ambitious!'

'I don't think you are at all,' said Rennie. 'If you ever do get to England you must look me up. I'll give you an address before we leave and we'll keep in touch.'

Jeanette's eyes lit up. 'That would be marvellous. Thank you so much.' She sighed wistfully again. 'I do so envy you, Rennie, sailing around the world with the Carmichaels. I only wish I could do the same. I adore sailing and I sail often with friends in my spare time, but I've never been very far, naturally.' She made a face. 'Nobody who calls here ever wants a nurse, or a nanny or even a deck hand!'

Rennie laughed. 'I'm surprised! I'd have thought all sorts of people would be jumping ship here, it's so beautiful and peaceful.'

Jeanette shrugged. 'I suppose it happens, but I haven't been lucky enough to hear of anyone needing someone like me. And besides,' she added ruefully, 'my parents wouldn't let me go with just anyone. They would be very particular.'

'I should hope so,' said Rennie. 'You need

to find someone like the Carmichaels. Perhaps you will one day, Jeanette.' She stood up. 'Well, I suppose we'd better not sit around here gossiping all morning.'

A couple of days later, Rennie, who had done a night shift, was off during the day, and in the afternoon she decided to take a leisurely stroll through the town. It was the first time she had done so and she found the experience very enjoyable.

There were tall Royal palms down the centre of the main street. There were a few shops and one or two office buildings, and at the far end of the thoroughfare, the road divided to encircle a vast botanical garden. Rennie spent a pleasant hour wandering through it, entranced by the unusual trees and shrubs, and the wealth of flowers. She had never seen orchids growing wild before, and stood looking in amazement at one delicate spray branching out from a tree trunk.

It was pleasantly cool in the gardens, although a little humid, but when she emerged the sun fell warmly on her bare arms and head, and she decided she ought to buy a hat. Seeing a sign pointing to a market, she set off down a side road and in a few moments found herself caught up in a bustle of tourists and locals who thronged the acre or more of stalls.

As she hesitated, wondering where to begin looking for hats, a hand touched her arm. She looked around and was astonished to see Craig standing beside her, smiling in quite a friendly way.

'Oh...hello,' she said, feeling foolishly disconcerted. He was the last person she had expected to see there. 'You're off duty too?'

'I'm never really off duty,' he answered dryly, 'but I had to come into town for a few things.'

'It's a charming place,' Rennie said. 'I've been walking in the botanical gardens. I've never seen such exotic flowers.'

'And now you are going to explore our market,' he commented, and then looking her over, added, 'You really ought to wear a hat. The sun is strong and we don't want you down with sunstroke.'

'As a matter of fact,' she said, 'I was about to buy a hat I was just wondering where to begin looking. There are so many stalls, and a lot of them seem to be selling straw ware.'

'I should be happy to show you around if you wish,' he said, giving her a quizzical look.

She wanted to refuse, but that would seem churlish, and in any case, a treacherous part of her wanted him there beside her, and that was the part that won.

'Well, if you can lead me to all the bargains...' she said lightly, to cover the confusion that his sudden appearance had aroused.

All the stallholders seemed to know him and by the time they had traversed all the long avenues of market stalls, Rennie had been introduced to practically every one. She found the hat in the first five minutes. They stopped at a large stall resplendent with basketware, carved wood, straw hats and sandals, and all manner of novelties. The big smiling Polynesian woman stallholder came forward eagerly when Craig told her that Rennie wanted a hat.

She brought out hat after hat and tried them on Rennie, who loved them all and could not make up her mind. Eventually Craig walked to a corner of the stall where more hats were hanging on a tall pole. He selected a broad-brimmed straw hat with a tall crown, swathed in yellow ribbon to which were attached many multi-coloured raffia flowers. He placed it firmly on Rennie's head and stood back.

'Yes, that's you exactly!'

The beaming stallholder clapped her hands. 'Yes, it suits you perfectly. The brim...' she moved her hands to describe the softly curving brim that was not as stiff as some of the others, '...it is so feminine!' She turned to

Craig. 'Your girl, she is beautiful!'

He just smiled enigmatically and said, 'Good, we'll have it. How much?' He took out his wallet.

'No, please...' Rennie protested. 'I'll pay for it.'

He waved her protest aside. 'No. I chose the hat, I'll pay for it.'

'But I don't want...'

The smiling stallholder was looking at her in some amusement as she fumbled in her handbag. Craig reached across and firmly closed it. 'It is a very small present, not worth making a fuss about. Accept it gracefully!' His eyes met hers and she felt her stomach turn. She didn't want presents from him. She didn't want to be under any obligation to him. She didn't want him to think...

He was already paying for the hat and then while the stallholder watched, still smiling, he caught the two yellow ribbons and tied them deftly under Rennie's chin.

'You don't want to lose it in the wind,' he said, as his fingers brushed her chin and sent electric shivers through her. They moved on, pausing at stall after stall as Rennie eagerly examined the wares, and bought several small items as souvenirs and to send home. Finally, Craig said, 'I could do with a cool drink, couldn't you?'

Rennie had to admit that she was thirsty. She suggested a lemonade at a nearby stall but he dismissed that with a peremptory shake of his head. 'No. The hotel is close by, and it will be cooler and less noisy in the garden there.' He glanced at her, 'You must relax whenever you can. You've worked hard these past few days.'

'Nurses do!' she rejoined spiritedly.

'Some more than others,' he remarked, but did not follow up the remark. Rennie wondered if he was making an oblique reference to Lilianne. He must be aware of her short-comings, she supposed, but if he was in love with her, naturally he would be generous with his tolerance.

They sat in a quiet corner of the hotel garden, shaded by a canopy of paw-paw trees and palms, and surrounded by colourful foliage and flowers. Rennie sipped a long cold lime drink and Craig had a lager. It was very peaceful there, and as Craig seemed disinclined to talk, Rennie remained silent. But she did not feel as relaxed as she might have done. She was too aware all the time of Craig's glances in her direction. Suddenly, from not wanting to talk about it at all, she longed to bring up the past and drag it all out into the open, to ask him about his wife and family, but even as she formed the opening words, her courage deserted her, and she leaned forward to take another gulp from her glass instead.

Craig drained his glass before she did, and looked at his watch.

'I'm afraid I'll have to go now,' he said apologetically. When she made to finish her drink too, he added quickly, 'No, take your time, there's no need for you to rush on your day off.' He rose and was gone with a quick backward lift of his hand, leaving her feeling slightly limp from the strain of the unexpected encounter.

She watched him weave his way between the tables and finally disappear from view, and although she felt a sense of relief from the tension of being with him in a kind of intimacy that was very unsettling, she also felt strangely bereft. That was a feeling she must be careful to avoid, she thought, gazing into the remainder of her drink.

'Rennie!'

Peta's voice broke into her thoughts and she looked up.

'I just saw Craig,' Peta said, 'and he told me he'd left you here.' She flopped down into the chair opposite Rennie. As she took off her own straw hat she spotted Rennie's. 'Hello, you've been to the market too!'

'Yes, just a short while ago. I met Craig there...'

'I love your hat!' said Peta twirling it. 'I love its floppy brim. It really is dandy. Where did you find it?'

'Actually Craig found it,' confessed Rennie, 'and he insisted on paying for it. I think he's feeling guilty for overworking me or something.'

'Has he been?'

'No. We've been quite busy but really it's a breeze compared to Whitehouse. You're dashing from one thing to another more here, that's the difference.'

'Must be stimulating,' observed Peta, 'or a man like that wouldn't stick it. I suppose that's what appeals to him, being in sole charge of the whole works.'

Rennie nodded. She did not want to discuss Craig at the moment, but the subject soon came back to him, after a waiter had materialised and Peta had ordered a drink for herself and insisted on another for Rennie.

She laughed and patted her cropped red hair. 'No prizes for guessing where I've been!'

'It looks terrific, said Rennie. 'Short hair suits you.'

Peta pulled a face. 'I hate hairdressers as a rule, but I felt it was getting a bit out of hand so I told her to lop it off. Do you really think it's okay? Brett will go berserk, but coping with longish hair is a nightmare on the yacht, and this will be so easy to care for.'

'I think Brett will love it,' said Rennie, thinking that the new short hairstyle made Peta's features more striking than ever.

'I had it set this time,' said Peta, 'but it's a wash-and-wear style—I hope! Ugh, it was ghastly sitting under the dryer, but guess who sat next to me?'

'I only know nurses,' laughed Rennie. 'Which one?'

'No. It was Isobel Anderson. She's quite a garrulous lady once she gets going, and she did this afternoon.'

'What about?'

'Craig mostly. Seems he's the apple of her eye as well as her daughter's. Do you know what she said to me, all confidential in a stage whisper, she said, "My dear, I'll let you into a little secret. We are expecting to welcome him into our family quite soon." '

Rennie caught her breath. So not only Lilianne was out to snare Craig, but her mother was too.

Peta went on, 'She's quite determined that her precious little Lilianne will marry him, but I hope he knows what they're up to.'

'He's pretty astute,' said Rennie dryly.

'I would think so,' agreed Peta. 'Do you think he's in love with her? You must have had opportunities to observe them together at the hospital.'

'I haven't really noticed,' said Rennie. 'He's always very professional in his attitude to the nurses.'

'I suppose he would be. I can't imagine him falling for a girl like her, though. I think she's a little prig. What's she like at nursing?'

Rennie answered carefully, 'She's rather inexperienced, but no doubt she'll learn. At the moment she tends to be a bit off-hand with patients and treats them like objects, not people.'

'That doesn't surprise me,' said Peta. 'Oh, well, I imagine he knows his own mind. He's a mature man. I suppose no man wants to remain a bachelor all his life and of course if he marries Lilianne he'll doubtless be able to twist her old man's arm for anything he wants for his hospital.'

Rennie was shocked. 'Surely he wouldn't marry her for that...'

Peta shrugged. 'He might. And she is very attractive, after all.'

'That makes Craig sound rather shallow,' protested Rennie. But wasn't he, she argued silently? Could any but a very shallow man have used her the way he had?

Peta said thoughtfully, 'I suppose we ought not to speculate. It's their private business.' She added thoughtfully, 'He's a rather deep sort of person, isn't he? He doesn't give much away—you can never tell what he's thinking just by looking at his face. I get the feeling sometimes that there's a lot more to Dr Craig Mackenzie than you see on that urbane surface he shows.'

Yes, thought Rennie, a wife and children for instance. Again she wondered if the Andersons knew about that, or was Lilianne in for the kind of shock she had suffered herself?

'What's Andrew doing today?' Peta inquired suddenly, changing the subject.

'Going over the sails, I believe,' said Rennie. 'At least that's what he said he was going to do this morning.'

'Poor Andy,' said Peta. 'He'll get very fed up with twiddling his thumbs once he's done all he can do on *Spindrift*. There's a limit even to how much maintenance you can do. Poor Brett, too, he hates being ill even for a day, and he'll be straining at the leash much too soon if we're not careful.'

'Craig's very pleased with his progress,' Rennie said, 'but he recommends convalescence for a reasonable time.'

Peta nodded. 'I know and I agree. I want to be getting on too, as I suppose you do, but we must be sensible. I've talked to Brett about it and suggested that as soon as he feels up to it, he starts drafting the book we're hoping to write about the trip. That will be useful work and it will stop him getting too fidgety.' She finished her drink. 'I'd better get back. Anna is wonderful the way she looks after the children, but I mustn't impose on her too much. Are you coming?'

Rennie nodded and they left together, walking slowly back to the hospital and Craig's house.

Rennie worked some night shifts and some day shifts and she fitted in so easily that sometimes it seemed she had always worked at Tavalei hospital. She was never completely at ease with Craig, but she managed to suppress her personal feelings most of the time and concentrate on the job in hand. Her fears that Craig might still try to revive their old relationship gradually faded and she no longer felt so on edge when she was alone with him. He was increasingly pleasant and friendly, and if he had borne her any grudge at the beginning because of hurt pride, he seemed to have got over it.

Whenever he dined with them all at the

house, he enlivened the mealtime with his stories of hospital life, both in England and on Tavalei, but always, Rennie noticed, he was close about his private life, and the only time he mentioned any family was to speak briefly about his aged father who lived in Edinburgh with his sister and her family. Rennie was not sure if she was imagining it or not, but she felt that a cloud passed across his eyes as he mentioned them, as though there was some deep hurt connected.

He touched once or twice on the time he had worked in London, but revealed nothing of his private life. If he was divorced, or even about to be, Rennie thought, surely he would have touched on it, if only briefly. There was nothing to be ashamed of and no-one was going to quiz him about whose fault it was. That he never mentioned his children was what really convinced Rennie he must still be living a lie and deceiving Lilianne as he had deceived her.

In her off-duty hours, Rennie sometimes took charge of the children, and invariably Andrew was around to suggest some excursion. Together they explored the island and occasionally took the yacht or the dinghy out for a day's picnicking on one of the small uninhabited islands that dotted the lagoon. Rennie enjoyed lying on the sun-drenched beaches soaking up the sun, swimming in the translucent sea, and if Andrew kissed her, she tried to respond with a little warmth, grateful because he never tried to take advantage of their time alone together.

Life on Tavalei, Rennie reflected often, was the kind of life you could insidiously become accustomed to. It was mostly blue skies and a mild temperature, with a not too unpleasant humidity. Showers were heavy but infrequent, and usually short-lived. While, in the morning, she could be dashing up to the hospital holding an umbrella over her head, by midday it would be fine enough for sunbathing again.

She felt herself adapting quite easily to the more leisurely attitude to life of the islanders. It had begun on the yacht, of course, where there had been long periods of inactivity when she was just minding the children and amusing them, when she had spent hours of companionable silence or conversation on watch with Andrew. Time had become meaningless for long stretches. But there had been periods of feverish activity too, such as on the night of the storm. After a while on Tavalei she began to feel that nothing could happen to upset the even tenor of their existence, but as always, just when one becomes complacent, something does happen.

The first Rennie knew of the emergency was when Craig burst into the pantry one morning where she was making a cup of tea for an elderly patient she had been reassuring about the haemorrhoidectomy she was due to have, after a spell of ineffective treatment for the condition.

'We've got to go out,' Craig said crisply.

Rennie immediately stopped what she was doing. 'Yes, what is it?'

'The supply lugger's just docked, and Captain Rilke sent an urgent message up. Old Klein—he's a hermit who lives alone on one of the small out-islands—gashed his leg a few days ago, and it's septic. The old man flatly refused to let them bring him over, so we'll have to go out there. Can you change into something suitable—slacks will do—and be ready in ten minutes?'

As he was speaking Lilianne came into the room. She had heard the news too.

'I'll come,' she said, with a sharp glance at Rennie. 'I know old Rolf...'

Craig shot her a cursory glance and cut her short. 'Not this time. I want Nurse Phillips to come with me.'

Perhaps he did not mean to be so crushing, but Rennie saw the resentment flood into the other nurse's face. Her eyes encompassed

118

Rennie with a flash of anger and dislike.

Craig, apparently unaware of the animosity he had just aroused, said briskly, 'Check my bag, Nurse Anderson, and tell Tommy to bring a stretcher.' Tommy was the Polynesian orderly.

He strode out and Rennie hurriedly went to find Jeanette to ask her to take the tea to the elderly patient. Then she ran down to the house, quickly changed out of her nurse's uniform into slacks and a cotton top, grabbed a cardigan in case she needed it, and fled back to the hospital. Craig, also changed, was on the verandah looking impatiently for her.

'Come on, let's go!' he said imperiously.

'How far is it?'

'About an hour's trip.' He was already striding ahead of her towards the car.

'What about Tommy?' she ventured.

'He's already taken the ambulance down to the quay,' he answered briefly.

Rennie was only mildly surprised to find that their transport was a motor launch. She slid into the seat beside Craig and almost before she had settled herself, Tommy was showing that he could handle a boat with the same bravura as he drove the ambulance. As they sped out across the calm blue water of the lagoon, Craig explained in more detail what had happened.

'Rolf Klein is an old man now,' he told her. 'He came to Tavalei when he was about fifty—twenty-five years or so ago, I believe.'

'Alone?'

'Yes. He was a lawyer apparently, back in West Germany, but he wanted to escape from the rat race and fulfil his dream of living on a South Sea Island.'

'That's what everyone seems to want to do nowadays.'

He glanced at her. 'You too?' there was a flicker of a smile on his tense mouth.

She shrugged, 'What about you?'

He laughed softly. 'We are all running away from something, I guess.'

The temptation to ask him then if what he was running away from was his wife and family was almost too much for Rennie, but it was hardly the moment to broach such a subject, even if she dared.

Most of the journey passed in silence. The launch engine was noisy and made talking difficult anyway. Rennie was glad when they finally beached on the crescent of white sand, tide-washed and unmarked by any human footprint.

'Where will we find him?' she asked.

Craig pointed up towards a rocky cliff. 'He lives in a cave up on the cliff. When he wasn't on the beach to take delivery of his supplies, the lugger captain went up to look for him.'

'It must be a bit risky living alone in a place like this,' said Rennie. 'Not as idyllic as you might imagine, if you have an accident or fall ill.'

Craig's face was grim and he did not answer as they walked across the sand and into the bush. Tall palms waved in the breeze, and cast a dappled shade across their path. Coconuts lay about in heaps on the ground and flowers were everywhere, but Rennie had little thought for the beauty surrounding her today.

Suddenly Craig said, as though there had been no long silence after her previous remark, 'So far he's been lucky, but apparently he slipped while fishing and gashed his leg on a sharp pinnacle of coral. Coral is often poisonous, and Captain Rilke said he's in a bad way.'

'He must be in considerable pain,' said Rennie.

'Rilke said he was delirious and it was difficult to ascertain exactly what did happen. They were afraid to try to move him by force.'

Rennie had to run a few steps every so often to keep up with Craig, and once they started climbing up the cliff she had no breath for speech, needing all her energy to keep up with him.

121

As they came to a ledge half way up the cliff, Craig called out, 'Hello, there, Rolf...it's Doc Mackenzie. Be with you in a minute.'

And then they were bending low and plunging out of the strong sunlight into the gloom of a deep cavern. At first Rennie could see nothing, but she almost gagged on the strong smell which hit them powerfully as they entered. It sickened her because, apart from the normal odours that were to be expected in a confined space where a man had lain helpless for days, there was the sickening one of gangrenous flesh.

Gradually, as her eyes became accustomed to the darkness, she saw the bundle of rags in the corner of the cave. Craig was already kneeling beside the old hermit.

'Rolf...' His voice suddenly cracked.

A limp hand rose from the covering blanket that probably the lugger captain had put over him. 'Doc...I'm okay...just a graze...' His accent was thick, the voice slurred.

'Sure thing,' said Craig, pulling back the blanket to examine the leg.

Rennie almost gasped aloud at what she saw. She hurriedly opened the medical bag and waited for Craig to ask for what he needed. He glanced at her and his expression told her the worst.

'I think the best thing we can do is to get you back to the hospital,' he said to the recumbent man. 'I can't fix you up properly here.'

The inert form suddenly contracted convulsively. *'Nein!'* the old man's voice was weak. *'Nein!'* he repeated more emphatically, and then broke into a torrent of German, mumbled incoherently.

When Craig tried to soothe him, he received no response. The old man had reverted to his native tongue and seemed unable to understand English now.

'Delirium,' said Craig, with another swift glance at Rennie.

She was kneeling next to the man's head, and suddenly realised he was saying the same thing over and over, *'Ich habe Durst...ich habe Durst...'*

'He's thirsty,' she said.

Craig started. 'You speak German?'

'Not really. I learned it at school and I spent one summer holiday with a family in Bavaria. I understand a little.'

For Craig that was enough. He called out, 'Tommy!' and the orderly who had been standing a little apart waiting for instructions came forward. 'Get some water, Tommy.' He had picked up a pannikin near the sick man that still had some in it. 'Tip this out, it's stale.'

He turned back to Rennie. 'We've got to get him out of here. I'll have to knock him out first though.' He turned away to fill a syringe, adding, 'Just try to reassure him.'

Rolf Klein stared vacantly at Rennie. She squeezed his hand and said, 'Rolf...*Ich spreche Deutsch...*

His eyes flickered. *'Fraülein...'*

'Is it very painful?' she asked.

He nodded, *'Ja...'*

'The doctor is going to give you something to ease the pain,' Rennie told him. 'Just a small prick in your arm, that's all.' Her recollection of German was hazy and she faltered over the words, but he seemed to understand.

His body convulsed again, *'Nein! nein!* Leave me alone!' He began to thrash wildly, and Rennie and Tommy had to hold him still. Rennie held the pannikin Tommy had filled to the old man's lips and he sipped some water. Rennie felt tears of compassion for the old hermit starting in her eyes, so she scarcely saw Craig swiftly inserting the needle into his arm. Moments later the old man was quiet, and they were able to move him.

Tommmy and Craig lifted him onto the stretcher and Rennie could see from the way they exerted very little effort that Rolf Klein was a very thin frail old man. Slowly they carried him down to the launch and gently placed him on board.

It was some hours later, when all that could be done for Rolf Klein had been done, and he was lying sedated in a small isolation ward, that Rennie, who was adjusting the intravenous drip above his pillow, ventured to say to Craig. 'How bad is he? There's gangrene, isn't there?'

He nodded. 'I'm afraid so. I don't think we can save the leg.' His lips were tightly drawn together and she knew he hated having to make such a decision.

'Can you, I mean will you amputate here?' she asked.

He nodded. 'He's in no condition at the moment to stand the shock. His heart's not too good. We'll have to wait a few days—if we can. I don't think it would be wise to try and transfer him. He's in a pretty weakened state and he's not young.' He eyed her steadily. 'You've assisted at amputations before?'

She swallowed hard. It was the kind of operation she liked the least. 'Yes.'

'Good.' She guessed he disliked the prospect as much as she did.

They had been tense hours and Rennie felt more exhausted at the end of that day than she had ever felt. She excused herself and went to bed early, but then found she could not sleep.

She tossed and turned for what seemed like hours. She heard Peta and Andrew come along the verandah and say goodnight, and then lay listening to the bursts of cicada song which punctuated the still, warm night. Eventually, feeling hot and sticky, she got up, realising she had forgotten to turn on the air-conditioner. Her finger was on the switch when she decided to go outside for a short while. Barefoot and without a dressing gown as it was so warm, she slipped quietly into the midnight garden. A stroll across the lawns and back, she thought, would be sure to induce elusive sleep, and the conditioner would have cooled her room down by the time she returned.

She strolled down the path towards the hospital. Jeanette was on duty tonight, she remembered. Perhaps she would just go in and chat to her for a few minutes and see how Rolf Klein was. Then she remembered she was only in her nightdress. She was about to turn back when a dark figure emerged from the hospital building and came down the side-entrance steps. It was Craig. He saw her before she could merge back into the shadows.

'Rennie! Is anything the matter?'

She felt extremely foolish standing there in her thin cotton nightdress, uncomfortably conscious of her nakedness beneath it, as his eyes roved slowly over her, and then met hers, looking for an explanation.

'I...was hot...I forgot to turn on the air-conditioner when I went to bed,' she said, stumbling over the words. 'I came out to cool off a bit.' She added quickly, 'How is Rolf?'

'It's touch and go...' He heaved a deep sigh and started to walk towards the house. She fell into step beside him, feeling there ought to be something else she could say but unable to think of anything.

Suddenly he stopped, and she halted too, glancing at him questioningly as he turned to face her. He looked down at her for a moment, and she sensed a tension in him that was near to breaking point. Then, without warning, he caught her roughly in his arms and held her against him, his face buried in her hair, and she could feel his heart beating against her through the thin material of her nightdress, his hands strong and warm.

'Adrienne...' he breathed. 'Do we have to behave like strangers?'

His eyes were pleading as they looked into her face, and Rennie felt her resolve weakening, her deepest feelings for him stirring once again and overtaking her good sense.

His mouth was on hers before she could resist, hungrily probing, parting her lips with his, and his arms were drawing her in against him, closer and closer, so tightly she could scarcely breathe.

'Craig...you said it wouldn't happen again...' Her faint protest was in vain. He did not hear, and her own feelings eventually drowned her resolve completely. For a long moment the past two years vanished in their entirety and this was as it had been before she had learned the truth about him. She was in his arms and there was nowhere else she wanted to be. She loved him and that was all that mattered.

Eventually he lifted his lips from hers, and gazed into her face, a faint smile lurking on his mouth. 'Rennie, I still can't believe you're really here. It's incredible, all these thousands of miles away and you...here!' He shook his head wonderingly, and one hand toyed with her hair, caressing the nape of her neck and then guiding her face closer to his again for another long, passionate kiss, presently sliding over her bare shoulder to cup her firm uplifted breast in strong demanding fingers. Rennie, her arms around his neck, pulled his head down to hers, intoxicated by the perfumes of frangipani and jasmine and other exotic scents of the garden, and overwhelmed by his nearness. She reckless-ly responded to him, wanting nothing except that this moment should go on forever. She was powerless to prevent her responses and the voice of reason was totally silenced in those moments of sheer bliss.

When he spoke it was to whisper her name, low and huskily, 'Adrienne...'

All the intensity of his desire was in that one word, and as she heard it, reality came crashing back. She pulled away from him.

'I think I'd better go back to bed,' she said in a flat little voice.

'No, not yet!' He gripped her shoulders, his fingers digging into the flesh of her arms which her nightdress was too skimpy to cover. 'Adrienne,' he pleaded, 'don't go...not yet. There's so much I want to say to you...'

She tried to steel herself against him, but her will was weak. All he wanted was to get her into his bed again, to take advantage of the feelings she had so foolishly just revealed to him. Or perhaps—her heart jumped erratically as she considered the alternative. Could it be that he was going to tell her he was free?

'Craig, I...' she began, hardly knowing what she was going to say, but her words were cut off before they were even formed. There was the sudden sound of a door slamming in the distance behind them.

They both turned and saw a figure flying down the pathway from the hospital, a figure they soon saw to be Kerri, one of the nurses. She did not notice them until she almost cannoned into them. She stopped, startled, and then breathlessly blurted out,

'I couldn't raise you on your alarm, Doctor, so I thought it mustn't be working properly,so I came...oh, please come quickly, it's Mr Klein...'

Without a word, Craig was gone, his long running strides outpacing the two nurses who ran after him.

CHAPTER FIVE

When Anna woke Rennie next morning her face was solemn. Rennie knew the reason why without asking, but she said:

'Anna, did he...?'

Anna nodded and a tear coursed down her plump brown cheeks. 'I'm afraid so, Miss Rennie.'

Rennie drew in a deep breath and let it out slowly. She felt as though a lead weight hung on her heart. Death was always like that, even when it was someone she did not know. It was sadness mixed with a sense of failure.

So Rolf Klein had died. She had expected it after last night's crisis. So had Craig. When she finally left the old man's bedside, ordered to go by Craig because he was going to stay there himself for the rest of the night, failure had been written all over his face. And Craig did not give up easily, she knew. Now she felt sad for the old man she had spoken to only briefly, but her heaviness of heart was also for Craig because she knew how he would be feeling this morning.

'He was an old man,' said Anna, twisting her apron between agitated fingers. 'He shouldn't have been living alone like that, but it was what he wanted. He wouldn't have it any other way. and Doctor Mac did all he could.'

Rennie nodded. 'Of course he did.'

Anna said, 'He told me not to wake you too early. You didn't get to bed until all hours.' She fussed about, straightening the counterpane which Rennie had hurled half onto the floor during her early tossing and turning, and then had not heeded later when she had flung herself down, more exhausted even than she had been earlier in the day. Unlike earlier, however, she had slept immediately.

'I'd better get up now,' Rennie mumbled, and seeing her breakfast tray, laden as usual, wondered how she was going to force the food down. Her one desire at that moment was to see Craig. She asked Anna where he was.

'He hasn't come back yet. He's still up there. I reckon he ought to get some sleep too. Maybe you could persuade him.'

Rennie nodded. 'I'll try.'

When Anna had gone she showered and dressed quickly, gulped down her orange juice, managed to eat a slice of toast and then washed it down with a cup of strong coffee. As she was about to leave, she suddenly caught sight of the pale blue uniform crumpled on the chair, and recalled what she had until this moment forgotten—her encounter with Craig in the garden. She had been clad only in her night-dress, and when Kerri had come she had raced back with her without even thinking about it. Now she recalled the odd look the other girl had given her, and the swift no-fuss way she had produced a spare uniform and quietly handed it to her at a suitable moment.

Kerri had not asked for any explanation as to why Rennie had been wandering in the garden at midnight with Craig, clad so flimsily, and Rennie had given her none. But as she was hurriedly pulling on the uniform, Lilianne, who had also come to assist with the patient, had looked at her curiously.

Rennie did not feel like talking and was glad when she did not meet anyone on her way up to the hospital. Peta and the children had gone out, so Anna told her, and Andrew was down at the yacht again, as he was most mornings, just to check on her and see what tasks needed to be done.

The hospital grounds were cool and fresh where the sun had not yet penetrated, but in the sunshine there was instant heat. Rennie screwed up her eyes against the glare as she

133

walked into the sun. On either side of her the hibiscus bushes flaunted a new crop of flamboyant flowers, yesterday's hanging closed and spent or already curled and dropped on the ground. An unseen bird called loudly from a concealed place, and the roof of the hospital shimmered in a heat haze, its whiteness reflecting the sun dazzlingly, as did the walls.

As Rennie entered as usual by the side entrance she encountered one of the nurses, called Cindy. 'Where is Dr Mackenzie?' Rennie asked her.

'In his office I think,' said the girl, and Rennie thought she gave her a rather odd, and not altogether approving look.

Rennie went straight to Craig's office. There was no answer when she tapped on the door so she pushed it open tentatively, half expecting him not to be there. But he was, seated behind his desk, slumped in the chair, his head on his chest, apparently asleep. Rennie tried to close the door quietly but it squeaked and he woke with a start and saw her.

'Rennie, come in!'

'Craig...I'm sorry, I didn't realise you were asleep.' She went in now, and he sat upright in his chair, looking a little dazed as he ran his fingers through his hair.

'Must have just dozed off for a minute.' He

regarded her steadily, his grey eyes expression-less. 'You know he died?'

'Yes, Anna told me. I'm sorry, Craig...' She walked over to the desk and he stood up and came towards her. He looked quite haggard.

He half sat against the edge of the desk, weariness in every line of him. 'It just wasn't possible to save him. We were a couple of days too late. His heart wasn't strong enough.'

She wanted desperately to fold her arms around him, and the need was so great she almost gave in to it.

'He was old, Craig,' she said, 'and the gangrene...'

He nodded. 'I know, there was nothing else we could have done, but...'

She smiled sympathetically, 'You always took it hard, losing a patient, didn't you?'

He didn't answer. She went on, 'Craig, you must get some proper sleep, or you'll be a cot case. Anna's worried about you...so am I.'

'You?' He let a smile play about his lips with faint irony.

'Everyone is,' she said, 'so go and get some rest, please.'

He ran his fingers through his hair again. 'But there's morning Surgery and...'

'I can handle that,' Rennie said firmly. 'I'll put off those I can't deal with myself, and I'll call you if there's any real emergency. With luck we might have a quiet morning.'

He stood up and linked his hands loosely around her waist. Her own rose automatically to hold on to him. 'You're a good girl, Rennie. I know I can rely on you. All right, I'll go. Any patients you can't deal with I'll see at three this afternoon. But first, there are a few formalities I must deal with—the burial, and notifying his next of kin. He was a widower and had no relatives except a cousin in Germany. Tommy's gone over to bring in his effects, such as they are, poor old guy.'

They stood for a moment, arms around each other, silent, looking into each other's eyes, and the only sound was the whirring of grasshoppers in the shrubbery outside the window, and the monotonous piping call of the unseen bird.

'We'll have to leave our talking until later,' he said. Rennie nodded. She was refusing to let herself think about that. She could only feel that somehow things were different between them.

There was another long pause, this time broken by the sound of the door opening. Instantly Craig's arms dropped to his side, and Rennie moved guiltily away from him. Lilianne stood in the doorway. Her dark eyes flicked from one to the other and showed they had registered the scene's intimacy.

'I beg your pardon, Dr Mackenzie,' Lilianne said in a chill, formal tone. 'I didn't realise you were occupied.' The door closed with a sharp click behind her as she retreated.

'I'd better get down to some work,' said Rennie, endeavouring to show no reaction to Lilianne's abrupt appearance and disappearance. Craig seemed unperturbed by it, or else he was just too preoccupied to realise that the girl had caught them in a rather compromising position.

He looked at her. 'Thanks for everything, Rennie.'

She went out, leaving him to the unpleasant task of arranging a funeral for the lonely hermit. The first patient she visited was Brett Carmichael. He had already heard about the night's crisis.

'I gathered something was going on last night,' he said, 'with all the rushing about. Poor old chap. Still, I suppose he had a good life, from his point of view anyway. He was living as he wanted to, doing what he wanted to do. Those of us lucky enough to be able to do what we want shouldn't complain.'

Rennie smiled. 'You're itching to get back to what you like doing best, aren't you?' She picked up his chart from the end of the bed and studied it.

He made a wry face. 'You bet. I hate being inactive, especially now I'm allowed up each day.'

'You mustn't take unnecessary risks, though,' said Rennie seriously. 'It's strenuous work sailing *Spindrift*, and don't forget you've a responsibility to Peta and the children.'

'That's right, lecture me! One more won't make any difference. You sound just like Craig! But don't worry, I'm not irresponsible enough to discharge myself until he gives the all clear. Though with Andy and you, I reckon I could convalesce on deck all day and just let you two run the boat.

'And who says we'd be willing!' said Rennie, glad to inject a little lightness into the morning.

He looked at her slyly. 'Do I detect a certain reluctance to leave this paradise?'

Rennie shook the thermometer vigorously. 'Well, life is very pleasant here,' she admitted. 'Peta is enjoying herself and so are the children.'

'But poor you are working, and Andy's as fidgety as a flying fish out of water.'

Rennie slid the thermometer into his mouth. 'Naturally, he's a bit restive. He can't wait to continue the voyage, but you mustn't let him persuade you to leave too soon.' After a moment she took the thermometer back and looked at it, smiling at him. 'Don't worry, Brett, it won't be for long.'

'Andrew's jealous,that's part of his trouble,' Brett said bluntly.

Rennie looked up sharply from writing on his chart. 'What do you mean?'

'Of you and a certain Dr Craig Mackenzie,' he said slyly.

Rennie felt her colour heightening. 'Oh, that's ridiculous.'

'Is it?' Brett's eyes danced wickedly. 'I understand you were found gallivanting around the garden with him last night, in your nightgown!'

Rennie hugged the chart to her, gripping it tightly, her face scarlet. So it was the subject of gossip already.

'That was because...' She saw that he would tease her unmercifully whatever she said. 'Oh, really!' she exclaimed, turning away to hide her confusion. 'Why people have to gossip...' She felt angry about it, and her tone conveyed her annoyance.

Brett said, 'Sorry, love, if I touched a sore point. Forget it. Your love life is your business, none of mine, or Peta's, but I'd like to know if I'm going to lose a valuable crew member.'

Rennie whirled back. 'You won't!' she said with emphasis. 'I've no intention of deserting the ship, skipper! I promise.' She meant it. Whatever Craig might have to say to her, it would make no difference. She would not let the Carmichaels down.

He laughed loudly. 'I reckon Andy would clap you in irons if you tried! He's a persistent devil when there's something he wants. He'll have a ring on your finger by the time we reach Southampton, I'll warrant, and I don't believe you're totally indifferent to him. I hope not, Rennie, because both Peta and I would be delighted to welcome you into the family. You're almost like one of us now, anyway.'

Rennie was deeply touched, and this added to her confusion.

'You've made me feel like one of the family, Brett, right from the start, all of you. I'd like very much to be one of the family officially, but—well, I don't know, we'll just have to see. Now, if you've got everything you want, I'd better get along. Craig's going off for a rest as soon as he can and I've got to cope with Surgery. See you later!'

She hurried out, somewhat disturbed by the conversation with Brett, and regretting now that she had not grabbed at least a dressing gown before going for her midnight ramble.

Rennie was in Outpatients, preparing for the first surgery patients when Lilianne came in. The girl stood stiffly in the doorway and regarded her with a supercilious air.

'Good morning, Lilianne,' Rennie greeted her pleasantly. 'I suppose you're a bit tired this morning too.' Lilianne would have had hardly more sleep than she had herself before coming on duty again. Yesterday's crisis had caused some disruption of the roster.

Lilianne, however, made no comment. 'You wanted me?' she said sullenly.

'Yes. I would like you to help me with Surgery. Craig has gone to get some rest.'

'I've got other things to do,' protested Lilianne unco-operatively.

Rennie clenched her teeth. Lilianne was obviously preparing to be her most difficult. 'If there's anything that can't wait, ask one of the others to do it,' she suggested curtly.

Lilianne tossed her head rebelliously. 'Who do you think you are, ordering people around? You're not in charge here, even if you think you are! You're not even a Sister!'

Rennie's cheeks began to glow with anger. This was no time for a tantrum, but with Craig out of the way, no doubt Lilianne thought she could get away with being recalcitrant. Rennie

141

was tempted to point out that she would have been a Sister had she not left Whitehouse General so precipitately. She remembered ruefully Matron's stern disapproval. At the time she had impetuously decided to give up nursing altogether, a decision she had later changed.

'Nevertheless, Craig requested me to see the out-patients this morning, and to ask another nurse to help me.' She met Lilianne's eye steadily. 'I don't think he would be very impressed to know you had refused without good grounds, and I would hope not to have to bother him in the circumstances.'

'What circumstances?' Lilianne asked.

'He had a difficult night, as you well know,' said Rennie patiently. 'We all did. We're all a bit on edge this morning, naturally. No-one likes a patient to die.'

Lilianne shrugged indifferently. 'I don't know why everyone's making such a fuss. People die all the time. He was only an old hermit.'

A great wave of anger welled up inside Rennie. 'That's just the sort of remark I'd expect from you!' she said, unable to control her disgust. 'Isn't there a spark of feeling in you for other people?'

Lilianne looked momentarily taken aback,

then she said, casually, 'You can talk. You cared so much you were flitting around the grounds in your nightie, just waiting to pounce on Craig!'

Rennie was so infuriated she took a step forward and her hand started to come up to slap the girl, but she managed to control herself, and taking a deep breath, she said, 'I think you have said quite enough, Lilianne. Would you please see that the examination table is ready. There don't seem to be any clean sheets.'

With a glance that indicated her triumph over Rennie, Lilianne did as she was asked, slowly and without the slightest enthusiasm, and her churlish attitude persisted throughout the morning.

As Rennie had hoped, it proved to be a quiet morning, with few patients for her to see. Fortunately no serious casualities turned up, and she had nothing more complicated to deal with than extracting a splinter, renewing a dressing on a cut arm, and giving an injection. One or two cases requiring diagnosis, and probably prescriptions, which she was not qualified to give, she sent away, feeling sure they were not urgent. She told them to return in the afternoon at the time Craig had appointed.

Throughout the day, her mind kept drifting back to last night and the moments when he had held her in his arms, and she had known she still loved him as deeply as ever. What was he going to say to her, she wondered, over and over? Was he just going to try and trick her again, or were the circumstances different now? Her heart beat faster at the thought that they might be, and yet even so she had doubts. Could she forgive him for deceiving her before? Did she really want a man who had deceived his wife? She knew that the only way to resolve her conflict would be to hear what Craig wanted to say.

There was no time that day for private conversations, and in the evening Craig seemed detached and pre-occupied. He made no attempt to see her alone. In fact, it seemed to Rennie all at once that he was at pains to avoid her. After dinner he went straight back to the hospital, and when she asked if there was anything he could help with, he answered with a curt, 'No.'

She went to bed convinced he had thought over last night, and now regretted his impulsive reaction. Perhaps he had decided there was nothing to say after all. There was, Rennie reflected, a factor she had allowed herself to forget temporarily—Lilianne.

The following day Rennie was able to take a day off, and when she encountered him on the verandah just after breakfast, Andrew suggested a picnic.

'You look weary,' he said, cupping his hand under her chin and looking at her with deep concern. 'You need to unwind.'

'I'm fine,' she lied, but admitted to herself that she was tense. 'But I don't think I feel like picnicking today, Andy.'

Andrew looked disappointed. 'I've already asked Anna to pack lunch.'

Rennie gave in. 'All right then. Maybe Peta and the children would...'

He cut her short. 'You've forgotten obviously that Peta is bringing Brett down here this morning. I think they might appreciate being alone, don't you? And you won't relax if we take the kids along. No, this time it's to be a lazy day for you.' He gave a sly smile. 'Doctor's orders!'

'Since when have you qualified?' she joked. His easy-going manner was having a relaxing effect already.

'Since now,' he said, and lightly dropped a kiss on her nose. 'Somebody's got to take care of you.'

'I can take care of myself.'

He shook her slightly. 'Maybe, but today I'm taking you off to a place called Pudding Island for a nice long laze on a deserted beach, and no arguments. Remember, I'm the skipper while Brett is laid up, and you're still on the payroll.'

'Heavens,' said Rennie, laughing. 'I am unlucky—two arrogant bosses to order me around!'

Andy was determined, and as Anna shortly appeared bearing a large picnic basket, and wished them a happy day, Rennie did not have the heart to refuse to go. She had no reason to feel uneasy about spending the whole day alone with Andrew on some deserted beach. He knew her feelings and would respect them, she felt sure.

They went in the dinghy, using the outboard motor, and Rennie really began to unwind as they sped away from the quayside. She looked back at their foaming wake, at the town gradually growing smaller and at once she knew that Andrew was right. She did need to get right away from it all, but not just for the reasons he supposed.

Pudding Island, the tiny coral atoll they headed for, was a mere dot, with a palm-fringed white beach encircling it, and dense bush covering most of its interior. They beached the dinghy and carried the picnic basket up into the shade of the palm trees. Then they went for a swim.

Andrew had brought snorkels and flippers for them both and they spent hours lazily observing the marine life of the coral reef that skimmed just below the surface of the translucent blue-green water.

Rennie became so entranced by the butterfly fish, the sea cucumbers, the rainbow fish, the many coloured corals and shells, the gently waving seaweeds that concealed all kinds of fascinating life, that she scarcely thought of anything else. It was simply perfect just lying on the surface of the water looking down into another world, occasionally moving her arms to shift position, but mostly remaining motionless as fish glided by unaware of her, or uncaring, or occasionally intrigued enough to bump their snouts on her goggles to see what strange creature lurked inside.

She might have stayed much longer, oblivious of time passing, if Andrew had not suddenly turned her over with a splash.

'Time for lunch!' he declared.

They splashed through the shallows to the beach, slipped out of their flippers and raced across the hot sand to where they had left the picnic hamper. Anna had done them proud. There was cold chicken and pork, paw-paw slices and mangoes, fresh bread, a salad and a bottle of white wine packed in ice.

'This is a feast for an army,' Rennie exclaimed, as she unpacked the food, while Andrew spread out the rug.

'We won't starve even if we get marooned,' he joked.

When they had eaten all they wanted, Rennie replaced the remainder in the hamper. They stretched out on the rug, content for the moment to remain in the shade as the sun was hot. Andrew reached for Rennie's hand and held it. She glanced at him uneasily, but his eyes were closed as though he meant to go to sleep.

However, after a minute or two, he said, 'How is Brett? Does this transfer to the house mean we'll be leaving soon?'

'No,' said Rennie. 'It's just that Craig thinks he'll be happier there. All he needs now is to rest for another week or two.'

'Another week or two!' Andrew exclaimed.

'You don't like staying in one place for too long, do you?'

He turned to grin at her. 'Nope.'

'But it's so beautiful here.'

'I know, but there are other places...'

'You're bored,' she accused.

He turned over and leaned on his elbows, looking hard at her. 'Yep. That's about the size of it. I'm fed up with dabbing paint on *Spindrift's* rails and polishing up the brasswork, and fiddling with the sails, and pottering with things that aren't the least bit necessary. I want to get moving again.'

A man always wanting to be on the move, thought Rennie. How would she like being married to such a man? Instinct warned her she would not. She was the kind to settle down and find her challenges in everyday existence. She would never have hared off around the world, she knew, if it hadn't been for Craig breaking her heart. She had enjoyed it, but it wasn't really her, not for always.

She said seriously, 'Andy, don't try to persuade Brett to leave too soon, will you? He's been quite ill, you know. Think of Peta and the children.'

He drew his lips together. 'I won't, don't worry, I'm not that irresponsible. I'll try to be patient.'

'How's your hand now?' Rennie asked, turning his palm up, noticing for the first time that she was holding the injured hand. There was just a strip of sticking plaster covering the gash now.

'Fine. It's healed nicely. That pretty little nurse—Jeanette something—took the stitches out for me yesterday.' He closed it around hers again and drew himself nearer to her. His face was close to hers and his lips were smiling. As he bent his head to kiss her, she knew suddenly that it was no use pretending, either to him or herself. She rolled away from him.

'No, Andy, not now...'

He let go and sat up. After a moment of uneasy silence, he said, 'I suppose it wouldn't be any use my asking you to marry me?'

This was so unexpected that Rennie was bereft of words for a moment, but as what he had said sank in, she knew that just the saying of it had answered all the doubts in her mind.

'No,' she answered quietly, 'it wouldn't be any use, Andy, I'm fond of you, but not in love with you. And don't hold out any foolish hopes that I might change my mind by the end of the voyage because I know I won't.'

'That's laying it on the line,' he said, his voice rather gruff.

'I'm sorry.'

He turned and smiled ruefully at her. 'I think I've known from the start I didn't stand a chance with you. No hard feelings, Rennie. I can stand being rejected.' He stood up and rather abruptly said, 'I'm going for a walk. Coming?'

'Would you rather be alone?' she asked, not moving.

He grinned, and his voice was more normal as he said, 'Come on! He held out his hand to help her to her feet. As she stood up he kept a firm grip of it, and gently shook it. 'We're shipmates, aren't we?'

'Of course,' said Rennie.

He dropped her hand and strode off down towards the beach. Stopping only to stuff their clothes and the rug hurriedly into the hamper, out of the wind, Rennie followed. She was a little shaken by the past few minutes, but glad it was at last settled between them.

'I reckon it'll take us about an hour to walk right round,' Andrew said as she drew level with him.

In the event it took much longer because in places the beach vanished and there were outcrops of rocks to clamber over. Rennie picked up pieces of coral that took her fancy, and collected shells, but although they laughed a lot, there was naturally some constraint between them.

They were more than half way back to the beach where the dinghy was when the clouds began to roll up swiftly, blotting out the sun.

'Hey, 'we're going to get caught in a down pour in a minute,' said Andrew, 'we'd better hurry.'

As they stumbled on over rocky places and ran along the springy sand, the sky became completely overcast and the wind strengthened.

By the time they reached the beach where they had picnicked, the first large drops of rain were beginning to fall, and lightning was rending the clouds, followed by deafening claps of thunder.

'We can't go back in this,' Andrew said, 'we'd better take shelter. It's going to be a storm.'

Rennie saw that the sea had quite suddenly changed from its peaceful blue to grey, and the lazy breakers that had been spreading fingers of foam across the smooth white sand were suddenly crashing furiously on the beach, sending fountains of spray up from the rocks, and splashing over the beached dinghy.

'I think we'd better pull the dinghy further up,' Andrew said worriedly. 'A squall like this could swamp it.'

They ran down towards it, and at the same moment there was a violent flash of lighting and a tremendous clap of thunder. Both sprawled on the sand, Andrew shielding Rennie instinctively.

'God!' he breathed a moment later, 'look what it's down to the boat!'

Rennie dared to look and saw to her horror that the dinghy was split almost in two. She turned to look at Andrew. 'Andy, it could have been us...' she whispered.

'Come on, we can't stay out in this,' he said. 'We'd better get up into the bush.' The rain was falling in sheets now, almost blinding then as they ran for the shelter of the trees, with the lightning cracking like whips over their heads and the thunder rolling across the sky like kettledrums.

'I thought it wasn't safe to stand under trees in thunderstorms,' Rennie gasped.

'Well, it's the lesser of the two evils so far as I'm concerned,' said Andrew. 'It could have been us out there instead of the boat.'

They huddled beneath a mango tree which afforded some shelter, and waited for the rain to stop.

'They'll be worried when we don't get back,' said Rennie at last. The rain showed no sign of letting up and it was beginning to grow dark in earnest now, not just because of the lowering sky.

'I told Anna we'd be back by six,' Andrew said.

'Perhaps someone will come over to see if we're all right,' said Rennie hopefully.

'In this sea, I think it unlikely,' said Andrew. 'Look at it!'

The sea was indeed rough, too rough for any small boat to venture out. Even if they still had the dinghy, Rennie realised, they would not

153

dare to try and return yet.

'We might be stuck here all night,' she said morosely, and shivered. Suddenly it was quite cool.

Andrew did not answer. 'We'd better get dressed,' he said.

Rennnie was glad she had stuffed their shirts and jeans into the picnic hamper so that they would not be blown away in the wind. They were as dry as anything could be expected to be, and the rug, too, was only slightly damp.

Andrew stood up and looked around. The rain was easing off now but there was no break in the clouds. He said, 'Let's go further into the bush. We might find some better shelter than this for the night.'

'Lucky for us Anna packed all that food,' said Rennie. 'At least we won't starve!'

She took one side of the hamper and Andrew the other, and together they picked their way along a kind of track in the gathering gloom. Suddenly Andrew stopped, peered ahead and said, 'Hello, what's that just ahead? It looks like a hut. Yes, it is! Come on.'

They ran the rest of the way, and burst into the hut jubilantly. It was made of palm thatch and had no door. It was in a state of disrepair but at least it afforded better shelter than just trees.

Rennie dropped her end of the hamper. 'Who's mad idea was it to have a nice relaxing picnic on a desert island?' she said, and they both burst out laughing.

'I only hope we don't have a tidal wave in the night,' said Andrew, and Rennie threatened to hit him.

'Let's eat,' she said, 'suddenly I'm starving.' There was a pile of palm fronds at one end of the hut, so they pulled some of them into the centre to cover the bare earth. There they sat and ate the remainder of their lunch while there was still just enough light to see. Fortunately they had not drunk the thermos of coffee at lunch time, and they were glad of that now.

'If we could light a fire they might see the smoke from Tavalei,' said Andrew. 'But I haven't got any matches.'

Rennie said resignedly, 'Well, they couldn't come and get us in this weather anyway, so we might as well make ourselves as comfortable as we can for the night. Someone will come looking for us in the morning.'

It was a long night. The storm passed but behind it came more continuous rain. It spattered through the leaking roof in many places, but they managed to huddle out of the way of it. They talked for a long while, told jokes, then

sang all the songs they knew, and finally
Andrew yawned and said:

'Well, this is all very well, but I'm tired.
Let's go to bed. We can pile on a few more
palm fronds, and with the blanket to cover us,
it might not be too bad.' He laughed suddenly,
ironically. 'I guess this might be the only time
I'll get to sleep with you!' Rennie's silence
made him add rather impatiently, 'You're not
going to be all modest and maidenly, are you?'

They could not see each other very well in
the darkness.

'No,' she said, a shade doubtfully.

'Oh, for heaven's sake, Rennie! I accepted
your decision, didn't I? But if you don't trust
me, you take the blanket and I'll curl up in a
damp corner somewhere. It's not really cold.'

Rennie bit her lip, glad he couldn't see her
face properly. She felt mean and unreasonable.
'I'm sorry, Andy,' she said, 'that was rotten
of me. Come on, let's try and get some sleep.
I don't want to be responsible for you suffering from exposure.'

They stretched out side by side on the pile
of dry palm fronds, and pulled the blanket over
them. It was far from comfortable but in spite
of it they eventually fell asleep.

Rennie was woken by a shout without at first
registering what it was. The world was full of

faint light once more. It was morning and the rain had stopped. Andrew's arm lay heavily across her, and he was still sound asleep. She stirred and sat up, and it was then she realised that someone else was in the hut, that what had awakened her was a shout—Craig shouting to Tommy, 'They're here!'

'Craig!' she cried with utter relief. 'Oh, thank goodness you've come,' but her thankful gaze met only a blank cold expression in his grey eyes.

CHAPTER SIX

As Rennie might have guessed, it was only Lilianne who made snide remarks about her night on the island with Andrew. When she came on duty the following afternoon, Lilianne was just going off.

'I trust you are none the worse for your adventure,' she said, putting a wealth of meaning into the final word. She looked Rennie over in her supercilious way.

Rennie ignored what she had said, and observed, 'I'm glad there was no damage on Tavalei as a result of the storm. It was very fierce.'

Lilianne shrugged. 'We often have storms. It was merely inconvenient for some people.' She smiled archly. 'Convenient for others.'

The remark hung in the air, and Rennie bit back the sharp retort she dearly wanted to make.

She was glad when Lilianne went. There were no innuendoes from Jeanette, and because of it Rennie felt herself warm to the young

158

nurse even more.

'I don't suppose you'll be here much longer,' Jeanette said, when Rennie commented on Brett's transfer to the house and his rapid improvement. She sounded almost wistful.

'We'll stay until Craig gives the all-clear,' said Rennie, 'but that shouldn't be long now. Brett's recovered very well.'

'Will you still be here for the Regatta?' Jeanette asked.

Rennie had heard mention of the Regatta but had forgotten exactly when it was to be held. 'How soon is it?' she inquired.

'Next weekend,' Jeanette told her. She added, 'You could enter *Spindrift* in some of the races.'

'Will you be racing?'

Jeanette shook her head. 'I don't think so. Unless someone asks me to crew. I haven't a boat of my own.'

'What about crewing with us?' Rennie said at once.

Jeanette coloured. 'Oh! I wasn't hinting...'

'I know you weren't. I'll talk to Andy about it. It would be fun, wouldn't it? We might even win a race!'

That night at dinner, she brought up the subject of the Regatta. Immediately Andrew's eyes lit up.

'What do you think, Brett? Could we race *Spindrift?*'

'By all means,' agreed Brett.

Andrew looked hopefully at Rennie and Peta. 'What about it, girls? Are you game to crew for me?'

Peta and Rennie exchanged glances. Peta's eyes sparkled excitedly. 'I hadn't thought of it, I must admit, but I'm game. What about you, Rennie?'

'I haven't had much experience,' Rennie said doubtfully, 'and none at all at racing.'

'Neither have I,' said Peta. 'But Brett and Andy have. They went in for the Admiral's Cup last year. Didn't win, of course!'

'Jeanette Raoul would jump at the chance to crew in *Spindrift,*' said Rennie. 'You might give her a chance, Andy.'

Andrew glanced at her. 'Sure, why not?'

Craig put in, 'The competition will be pretty stiff. Yachting enthusiasts come from all over. Tavalei will be bursting at the seams again next weekend.'

Brett said hopefully, '*Spindrift* is a good boat of her class. Not primarily built for racing, of course, but she's speedy, with lots of pluck. We might just fluke a ribbon!'

'Or get a gold medal for glamour!' said Andrew, with a mischievous grin at the girls.

He switched his attention to Craig. 'Any chance of Brett proving his fitness?'

Brett flexed his muscles. 'I'm feeling pretty good.'

'You must do what Craig says,' put in Peta doubtfully. 'You don't want to undo all the good work.'

'All right, I'll just watch,' said Brett resignedly.

Craig, however, said, 'I was not going to forbid you taking part, Brett. As a matter of fact I think you might as well have a work out and see how you go.

Even Peta looked surprised, and later she said to Rennie, 'You know, Rennie, I've a feeling we've about worn out our welcome. I think Craig is suddenly quite keen to get rid of us.'

Rennie had been thinking the same thing. She was in a quandary over Craig. He had said a few nights ago that he wanted to talk to her, and yet he had made no opportunity for it. She wondered if it was because of Andrew. He no doubt believed the worst of their night on the island. She wanted to explain it to him, but apart from there never being a suitable opportunity to broach so delicate a subject, she was not sure it would be wise to do so. She did not know what Craig had wanted to say to her, and she knew that it was foolish to have hoped he meant to tell her he felt more for her than a passing passion. She had half believed he had changed his mind the next day in any case. Perhaps if she had been surer what his relationship with Lilianne was, she might have been braver about taking the initiative, but as it was pride kept her from speaking.

Every spare minute during the next few days was occupied, either preparing *Spindrift* for the Regatta, or training. Jeanette joined the team and Rennie quickly realised that the girl was a far superior seawoman to her. She pointed this out to Andrew.

'Andy, you don't really need me, do you? Jeanette's a much better sailor than I am.'

Andrew had looked uncomfortable. 'Well, she's had a lot more experience, but you're pretty good.'

'Not for racing,' maintained Rennie. 'I think you'll stand a better chance in the races you've entered without me. Stick to Peta and Jeanette and you'll probably win. I bet Brett will agree with me.'

His face broke into a relieved smile. 'You're a brick, Rennie. Thanks!'

'Don't mention it,' she said. 'I'm sure I'll have just as much fun cheering from the dinghy!' She added teasingly, 'Which I trust will be quite seaworthy again by then!'

162

Andrew's enthusiasm knew no bounds, and one evening at dinner he announced that he had come to an arrangement with a friend of Jeanette's to race his yacht as well as *Spindrift* in the Regatta.

'It's a really sleek racing yacht,' he said. 'She's a joy to handle.'

'Why isn't he racing her himself?' asked Brett.

'He's sprained his ankle. But she's practically a new boat so he's anxious to see her put through her paces.'

The days leading up to the Regatta were hectic, and became more so towards the end. Rennie valiantly worked longer hours so that Jeanette could have more time off during the day for practice. The young nurse protested strongly about the unfairness of it, but Rennie insisted. She was anxious for Brett and Andrew to do well in *Spindrift*, and she also hoped Andrew and Jeanette would win with the borrowed yacht. Once, going to watch them practise, she noticed the way Andrew looked at Jeanette, the way his eyes skimmed over the slim pretty nurse who, out of uniform, in shorts and T-shirt, or bikini, proved to have a very shapely and attractive figure. Andrew obviously appreciated what he saw. Rennie thought ruefully that it was a pity they would soon be leaving. Andrew could do worse than fall for a girl like Jeanette.

She felt very restless herself now, and eager to move on. Working with Craig was becoming intolerable. On the surface there seemed to be no change, but to Rennie there was something difficult to define in his manner. Whereas, for a time, she had thought they were moving towards understanding, now they seemed further apart than ever. She would never know what he had wanted of her.

The Regatta however made a welcome diversion, and no-one was more pleased than Rennie when *Spindrift* won a race for her class and came third in an open contest. And she almost fell out of the dinghy cheering when Andrew and Jeanette just pipped the leader over the line racing the borrowed yacht.

There were celebrations all over the island that night. The Carmichaels, Andrew and Rennie, together with Jeanette, were invited to the hotel for the festivities there. Rennie and Jeanette shared their shift that night because Jeanette would not hear of Rennie missing all the fun.

'You've been too good to me already,' she said, her dark eyes shining. 'I've never had such a wonderful time!'

Rennie bit her lip. She was sure that a large

part of Jeanette's gaiety was due to Andrew. She hoped she would not be too heart-broken when they all left.

And that was to be sooner than even she expected, Rennie discovered next morning. After only a few hours sleep, she was on her way to the hospital again, when she encountered Peta on the verandah.

'Rennie, good news!'

'What?'

'Craig said last night that we can leave anytime now. He's going to give Brett a final check today, but he says there's no reason why we can't go right away. Brett feels great, even after yesterday, and he actually says he's glad he didn't try to move too soon. I think he's enjoyed himself here almost as much as we have! And he's done quite a bit of the book.'

Rennie knew she ought to be as thrilled and excited as Peta, but she wasn't. Why wasn't she? There was nothing for her here on Tavalei except heartbreak.

She walked slowly up to the hospital, and, as she entred, Craig came along a corridor.

'Ah, Rennie.' His eyes met hers, but without expression. 'Come into my office for a momment, please.'

She followed him in, her heart hammering. Was this going to be the long-delayed moment she had been waiting for?

He did not ask her to sit down but stood a little apart from her, gazing for a moment or two out of the window, then he turned back and said, 'I'll be seeing Brett for a final check up today. I've already told him he's fit to leave anytime, so I imagine you'll be leaving in a few days. I'm sure you'll be glad to be on your way again.'

'Yes,' she said, and her heart suddenly felt as though he had taken it in his hands and torn it in two. 'Yes, of course, but...'

He anticipated her by saying, 'It's working out wonderfully well. I've just had a cable from Sister Donaldson. She'll be back in a few days.' He paused, arms folded across his chest. 'I'd like to say here and now, Rennie, how grateful I am for your help these past few weeks.'

'Please don't...' She wanted to run now, not be forced to stay in his presence. She glanced at her watch. 'I'm late already. There are the medications to see to...'

She was about to ask him for the drugs-cupboard key when he said, 'Lilianne has the key. I gave it to her some time ago.'

Lilianne. She always had to intrude. Briefly there flashed through Rennie's mind a picture of her last night, flushed and excited, dancing a wild rhumba with Craig, and his face had

166

seemed all lit up too.

There were, Rennie supposed, things she should have said about how much she had enjoyed working in the hospital, seeing Craig again, but she said none of them. Perhaps she would summon enough composure to do so before she finally left, but this morning as she had suddenly discovered, her emotions were too close to the surface.

She concentrated her mind on her work, and walked purposefully along to the small dispensary. Lilianne was there.

'Sorry I'm late,' Rennie said. 'I hope nobody's been complaining. I stopped for a word with Mrs Carmichael and then Craig buttonholed me.'

Lilianne treated her to her usual supercilious smile. 'The world turns without you,' she said.

Rennie took a deep breath. Thank goodness she soon wouldn't have to put up with this girl. 'All right,' she said, 'let's make a start...'

Lilianne did not move. 'You needn't bother. I've already given them all.'

Rennie stared. 'You've what?'

'You were late,' said Lilianne. 'I didn't know whether you were coming in or not, so I got on with it.'

For a moment Rennie was dumbfounded. Then she found her voice, which she managed to keep level with difficulty. 'Who checked you?'

Lilianne tossed her head. 'No-one.'

Rennie blew up. 'Lilianne, surely you know that you don't prepare medications and administer them alone. There must always be someone to check and sign the record book with you.'

Lilianne thrust out her bottom lip rebelliously. 'Well, there wasn't anyone around, and I've done these enough times.'

'You know the rules,' said Rennie. 'There was no reason to break them. A few minutes wouldn't have made any difference.'

'Oh, for heaven's sake,' said Lilianne, 'don't make such a fuss about it. It's done and that's all there is to it. You ought to be grateful. You weren't here, so someone had to do it.'

'I think you should at least have consulted Craig,' said Rennie. She was sure he would consider her action a serious breach of hospital rules.

Lilianne faced her resentfully. 'Now I suppose you'll go and tittle-tattle to him. You're always trying to ingratiate yourself with him, aren't you? Pretending nobody knows as much as you do. You're not content to have Andy on a string, you want Craig too. Well, it won't work. He's awake up to you!'

'I will not tittle-tattle as you put it,' said Rennie carefully, 'but I would suggest that in future if the same situation should arise, you tell him what you intend to do before you do it.'

'He gave me the key to the drugs cupboard when I asked for it,' Lilianne said airily.

'That didn't constitute permission to administer medications without supervision,' said Rennie sharply. 'I think you should remember, Lilianne, that as nurse you hold a position of great responsibility. There are a number of people entirely at the mercy of us nurses for their recovery and well-being.' She had not intended to lecture the girl but she was infuriated by her stubborn arrogance.

Lilianne's eyes flashed. 'Oh, you make me sick!' she exclaimed. 'I'll be glad when you're gone. I'm sick and tired of you being here. We don't need you to tell us what to do!' On those words she flounced out, while Rennie clenched her fists and then banged her knuckles ineffectually but rather painfully together. Lilianne Anderson was the giddy limit. And Craig was stupid enough to want to marry the girl!

As Lilianne went out, Kerri, another nurse, came in. 'Dr Mackenzie says can you come right away,' she said. 'He's starting Surgery early as there's rather a crowd already.' She grimaced sympathetically.

It proved to be a hectic morning. The Outpatients waiting room was full from the start, and Surgery ran well over time. With two new admissions demanding her attention immediately afterwards, Rennie did not accompany Craig on his morning round of the wards as she usually did when she was on duty, but left it to one of the other nurses.

She was too busy to think about Lilianne, but when she returned to the Duty Room to find the girl staring absently out of the window she almost lost her temper.

'Is that all you've got to do?' she exploded. 'Nobody else has time to stare out of the windows!'

Lilianne turned. 'Oh, get off my back,' she said insolently.

'Lilianne...' Rennie had had just about enough, but before she could say any more, Craig burst into the room, his face dark with anger. Even Lilianne looked taken aback.

'I want to know,' he demanded in a furious tone, 'why Mrs Garrett did not have her insulin injection this morning.'

Rennie let out an involuntary gasp and glanced at Lilianne, who at least had the grace to flinch guiltily.

'She hasn't gone into a coma has she?'

Rennie ventured, appalled. Mrs Garrett was a recently diagnosed diabetic and Craig was still determining the correct dosage for her.

'No, but that is beside the point!' he thundered. 'I want to know why she was missed.'

Rennie glanced at Lilianne again, who momentarily looked apprehensive. It was foolish, she knew, but Rennie suddenly felt sorry for the girl. She was young, inexperienced and a bit headstrong. if she told him that Lilianne was responsible, Rennie thought, Craig would certainly vent his fury on her, regardless of their relationship. Lilianne deserved a dressing down, even from the man she hoped to marry, but Rennie hesitated.

'Well...' said Craig ominously, 'I'm waiting for the answer, Nurse Phillips.'

Rennie bit her lip. But before she could say a word, Lilianne spoke, hesitantly, almost apologetically.

'I...I administered all the medications this morning, Craig.'

Rennie stared at her, unable to believe she was actually owning up to what she had done. She must know he would be angry, or was she sure she could twist him round her little finger over anything? Then, as Rennie stared, Lilianne went on sweetly:

'Nurse Phillips was a bit late, so she just made them up and told me to get on with it. I've done it so many times before, but I thought it was a bit odd about Mrs Garrett, but Nurse Phillips is in charge. I suppose I should have said something, but, well, she doesn't like you to query her...'

Rennie almost fainted. The effrontery of the girl, thinking she could get away with it! She glanced at Craig, and the words she had been about to use to expose the barefaced lie died on her lips. He expression was grim.

He said acidly, 'It seems your mind was on other things this morning, Nurse Phillips. I know you won't be here much longer, but I would appreciate it if you didn't let your love life intrude into your work.'

His tone was so cutting, so hurtful, and so humiliating that she could not answer. Lilianne looked triumphant. Craig was, of course, much more willing to believe her than Rennie. and if he bothered to look in the record book he would see that her signature was not there, and assume she had forgotten that too. But she was to blame, she thought guiltily. She should have insisted on double-checking what Lilianne had done, but Lilianne had flounced out and Craig had summoned her to Surgery.

Her immediate reaction was to tell Craig that

she would leave the hospital immediately, but she was not going to do it in front of Lilianne and give the girl that satisfaction. If Craig wanted her to go, then it was up to him to say so. She waited but he said nothing, just looked at her, then turned on his heel and walked out. The moment he had gone Lilianne followed and Rennie was still too stunned to stop her.

Several times during the day she was tempted to have it out with Lilianne, but she knew that losing her temper with the girl would achieve nothing, and only make her all the more antagonistic. What really rankled most about the affair was that Craig, who had always held her in high regard professionally, had so readily accepted the slur on her competence. She felt miserable.

How Rennie got through the rest of the day, she scarcely knew. It was close to the end of her shift and the minutes were dragging, there suddenly being very little for her to do, when she passed Craig's office on her way to check with the laundry over some missing linen. The list she was holding suddenly slipped out of her hand, and as she bent to retrieve it, she realised that Craig's door was slightly open because she heard Lilianne's voice quite distinctly. To her surprise the girl sounded tearful.

So astounded was she to hear the normally

self-possessed Lilianne in tears that Rennie paused and listened without thinking.

'...it's all her fault,' Lilianne was whimpering. 'Everything was great until she came along and spoilt it...'

'She hasn't spoiled anything, Lilianne,' Craig's voice was low, conciliatory.

'She has! I don't know what you see in her, Craig. It's obvious what sort of woman she is. Look at the way she carries on with Andrew Barker. They aren't even discreet!'

'Lilianne!'

'Well, you'd have to be naive not to guess what she was doing gadding about the garden in her nightie. She sneaks down to the bungalow every night, you can bet, and I'm sure you don't believe that night on Pudding Island was babes-in-the-wood stuff!'

There was a low laugh from Craig. 'You sound as though you're jealous.'

'I am!' replied Lilianne heatedly.

'Don't tell me you've fallen for Andy?' he teased.

Lilianne exploded. 'Don't be so infuriatingly obtuse, Craig. You know perfectly well it's you I love. I'd have an affair with you any time you want, you must know that, and I thought you were interested in me—but since she came, everything's changed, you've changed...'

He did not answer for a moment and Rennie was about to move away, looking guiltily around in case anyone noticed her eavesdropping, when his voice came again, gentle and soothing.

'You're a silly child, Lilianne. You've got it all mixed up. Nothing has changed at all. Everything is exactly as it was before, I assure you, including me. Now, come over here and sit down. We need to have a good heart to heart talk and straighten this all out...'

Their voices faded. Rennie remained frozen to the spot for a moment more as she pictured them moving across the room to the big leather couch, sitting side by side, Craig gently reassuring Lilianne.

CHAPTER SEVEN

'I would like you to come on the out-island run with me tomorow,' Craig said brusquely to Rennie the next morning.

Rennie looked up from the sterilizer in which she was placing instruments. She had not heard him approach, and now wondered uncomfortably how long he had been standing there watching her. Yesterday's debacle was still vividly imprinted on her mind, as was that subsequent interview with a tearful Lilianne which she had overheard.

'What time do we leave?' she asked, keeping her voice as level as her emotions allowed.

For some reason he looked extraordinarily handsome this morning, in his crisp white coat, his dark hair brushed back from his broad forehead, and in spite of the hard, uncompromising line of his jaw and unsmiling mouth. Loving him, she thought, was a chronic disease. There was no cure for it. Whatever he did to her, however he treated her, he still had the power to turn her feelings upside down just by being there. She could only feel glad now that she had had the strength of will not to fall back into their old relationship at his bidding, to be his temporary love again. If Lilianne was so willing, she thought fiercely, why didn't he have an affair with her?

After what seemed a long interval, Craig answered her question. 'Early. Eight o'clock. We may have a busy round, we may not. I go once a month. It's easier than people having to come here to have minor ailments treated. There are only four islands to visit. Most of the out-islands are uninhabited.'

'How do the people live?' Rennie inquired, interested.

'They grow coconuts and paw-paws and other fruits, a bit of vanilla. They fish, of course, but copra is the mainstay.'

'You'd better let me know what you require in the medical kit, other than standard items,' Rennie said, averting her eyes from his, as she closed the sterilizer and switched it on.

'We'll go over it together later,' he said, and walked out as abruptly as he had come in.

The next morning Rennie viewed her day with some apprehension. In the hospital, she did not have to see Craig every minute of the day, but today she would be with him all the time. She knew it would be a strain. She was ready and waiting before he was, to ensure that their day did not begin on a wrong note, and she had checked and double-checked the medical kit to make sure there were no omissions from the list he had given her.

Lilianne had looked rather sullen when she realised that Rennie was going on the out-islands trip. Clearly she had expected to go instead, assuming perhaps that because of Rennie's supposed lapse of efficiency two mornings ago, Craig would have been reluctant to take her.

'Sister Donaldson always went with him,' Jeanette assured Rennie, after Lilianne had made some oblique remark suggesting she was the one who ought to have gone, and that Rennie was pushing herself in.

'We'll be away all day,' Craig said as they got into his car to drive down to the harbour. 'This is the day I pray no crisis occurs, although the hospital can get in touch with us by radio if anything drastic should happen.'

Rennie had assumed that they would be travelling in the motor launch, and so she was surprised when they walked along the quay to find that this was not so. Craig pointed to the small seaplane bobbing on the lagoon a short distance from the shore. 'There's our transport for today.'

'You didn't tell me we were flying!' Rennie exclaimed.

He glanced at her. 'Didn't I? Sorry. I assumed you would realise the islands are a bit far for the launch. The plane saves us a lot of time. It's Anderson's. He does a lot of island hopping himself, and uses it for spotting fish shoals, too.'

'Mr Andeson seems to be into everything,' remarked Rennie, as Craig helped her down into the dinghy where a beaming Tommmy steadied her.

'You sound as though you don't care for him much,' said Craig, mildly reproachful.

Rennie wished she had not spoken. She had nothing against Alan Anderson. She liked him, in fact, and he was doing a lot for Tavalei. It was his daughter she disliked, not him. She was edgy with Craig, that was the trouble.

As the dinghy putt-putted out to the plane, her thoughts suddenly ranged back in time to the days at Whitehouse General when her relationship with Craig had been so different. She could not help remembering how rapidly their friendship had deepened from casual conversations in the canteen, meetings at staff functions, to occasional outings together, and then to quiet evenings at her flat, which Craig had seemed to like best.

It was the one place, he had always said, where he could relax and find solace. To look back on those times, that idyllic six months during which friendship had turned to deep love, on her part, was agony. She wondered if he ever thought about it. Probably only in passing if at all. It had not meant as much to him as he had pretended, or she had believed. She had been a fool to read more into their relationship than he had intended.

The pilot of the plane was the Anderson's son, Theo. He greeted them cheerfully, and welcomed Rennie aboard. Craig handed her up from the bobbing dinghy, and again the firm touch of his hand on her bare arm sent a shockwave through her as it always did. She settled herself in her seat, stowing the medical kit where Theo indicated, as Craig waved Tommy off and closed the aeroplane door and fastened it. He sat beside Rennie, and noticing she had not fastened her seat belt, leaned across to do it for her.

'All right?' he asked, glancing solicitously at her. 'You look a bit pale.'

'I'm fine, thanks,' she answered. Any shakiness she was experiencing was not at the prospect of flying in a light plane for the first time, but simply because his nearness was disconcerting her more than she should have let it. He was in a softer mood this morning. No doubt because everything was resolved with Lilianne, Rennie thought bleakly.

'Theo's a first-rate pilot,' he assured her. 'You've nothing to worry about.'

'I'm not worried!' she retorted.

'Oh...' He seemed to flinch a little. 'I thought maybe this was your first time in a small plane, especially a seaplane.'

'It is, but that doesn't mean I'm scared.'

'Sorry,' he said, with a laconic lift of his brows.

Rennie concentrated her gaze out of the small window through which the water looked very close. The engines of the tiny plane revved, filling her ears with a harsh roaring, as they began to move forward, churning the water as they gathered speed. Spray blotted out her vision temporarily as the floats skidded effortlessly along the surface of the water. Finally they parted from the water like sticking plaster wrenched off skin, as the aircraft became airborne.

Almost immediately the slipstream cleared the water from the windows and briefly there was Tavalei spread out below, an exotic panorama of white beaches with deep green palm trees fringing the shoreline, and mingling with the denser forest of the interior. Here and there Rennie glimpsed the clearings that were villages.

They circled once around the island as they rose higher, and then headed in a westerly direction. Tavalei was rapidly left behind, but below them stretched the lagoon with myriad small islands seeming to bob on its surface like marker buoys. These atolls were pinnacles of the coral reef, some adorned with only a few palms. One that Rennie noticed sported rather comically only a solitary palm on its minuscule projection.

The scenery temporarily diverted her attention from Craig, but once when she glanced aside at him she saw that he was as engrossed as she was with the view from the window on the other side. In only a few minutes the plane was dropping down towards the water again, there was a gentle thump and a splash, and they were skimming lightly over the surface towards a palm fringed shore. Through the windscreen, over Theo's shoulder, Rennie saw figures moving on the beach, and bobbing about in canoes a short distance out from it. They came to a halt within a few yards of a large native outrigger, to which they transferred for the last few hundred yards to the beach.

Beaming smiles greeted them and, chattering animatedly, a dozen or more men, women and children, surrounded by barking dogs, escorted them up the beach into the village. Surgery was held in a large open thatched hut where the patients sat in a row on the ground and waited patiently for their turn. The only privacy was a screen woven of pandanus leaves around the examination table.

There were not very many patients to see and there were no serious cases to deal with, to Rennie's relief.

'As you can see, it's chiefly a matter of dispensing aspirin and antiseptic!' remarked Craig once in a moment's respite between patients. 'They're basically a healthy lot.'

Surgery over, they were invited to have morning tea at a nearby house.

'Every family takes a turn to entertain the doctor,' whispered Craig to Rennie as they walked through the dust to the house in question.

Rennie, as a newcomer, was welcomed with some ceremony, and a lei of frangipani and hibiscus blossoms was placed around her neck. She was also presented with a colourful hand-woven basket decorated with raffia flowers by the lady of the house who, together with several other women, was engaged in making them for sale in the market in Tavalei. Rennie lingered for some time watching them at work and asking them about their craft, fascinated by the adept way they split and wove the palm strips.

As they were leaving, a small boy with a bandaged foot hobbled forward and presented Rennie with a large shell of unusual shape, its fragile spines a brownish pink colour. She recognised him as the youngster out of whose festering foot Craig had extracted a sharp fragment of coral. Rennie had bandaged it for him afterwards. This was evidently his way of saying thank you. Very touched, she bent and kissed him. He scurried away as fast as his injured foot would allow, giggling convulsively.

'Diving for shells like that to sell to tourists is how he cut his foot,' Craig said.

As they were again settling themselves back in the plane, having been accompanied to the beach and waved off by the whole village, Rennie could not help saying impulsively, 'What delightful people they are! I'm not surprised you love living on these islands.'

Craig shot her a sidelong look and a smile. 'They thought *you* were delightful!' There was a softer expression in his eyes than she had seen for some time.

She blushed. The compliment was unexpected, but she thought sincere.

Their treatment was exactly the same on the next island they visited, and Rennie began to feel embarrassed with the gifts she was receiving. Craig and Theo both assured her that it was usual for a newcomer to be thoroughly welcomed in such a way.

At their third stop they were given lunch, and having become accustomed to Anna's lavish spreads, Rennie was hardly surprised when she saw the long bamboo trestles, covered in green banana leaves and loaded with all kinds of delicacies.

'It's a feast!' she exclaimed.

'The women will have been preparing this all morning,' said Theo beside her, 'so flatter them by eating well.'

'It's just as well you only come once a month,' Rennie remarked to Craig. 'This would wreck any diet!'

He laughed. 'You needn't worry about your figure. There's nothing too fattening here. Here, have one of these.'

'What is it?' Rennie took a piece of the strange looking substance he offered.

'Fish.' He popped a piece in his mouth and ate it.

Rennie did the same. 'Mmm, it's quite nice,' she said, not certain whether it really tasted as fish should taste. 'What sort of fish is it?'

His eyes were twinkling, 'Octopus!'

Rennie grimaced. 'Ugh!'

He laughed. 'You just said it was quite nice! Have another piece.'

Rennie drew back. 'No...I don't think I will, thanks. I like the look of those paw-paw slices better.'

Presently Rennie found herself sitting along with Theo, both having had enough to eat, and now leisurely sipping cool fruit drinks. Craig was talking to a group of men on the other side of the luncheon table.

'You evidently like the life out here?' Rennie remarked after a silence. Theo was not a talkative person, but he was not standoffish, she felt, just rather shy.

He turned to smile at her. 'Suits me. I'm my own boss virtually. Dad gives me a pretty free hand.'

'Craig said you were inspecting the copra plantations,' Rennie said. Theo had disappeared at each stop, driven off in a landrover, and when she had commented, Craig had said that he was there on business.

Theo nodded. 'That's right.' And then, to Rennie's surprise, he launched into a detailed description of his work as his father's right-hand man in the diversified business of Alan Anderson and Son. He told her about the copra business, their fishing ventures, the fruit

186

packing and exporting, and their planned tourist expansion.

'Tavalei has got a lot going for it,' he told her. He was obviously a man dedicated to his chosen way of life and his enthusiasm was infectious. Rennie felt she had learned more about the islands during half an hour talking to Theo than she had since she had been on Tavalei.

Finally he stood up, saying apologetically, 'I must excuse myself, Rennie, I'm afraid. I've got work to do before we press on.' Abruptly he was gone. Rennie watched him gather several men around him, talking animatedly, and as they disappeared, Craig appeared at her side.

'Feel like a walk? We won't be moving on for an hour or so. Theo's got some business to do.'

Rennie stood up. 'Whatever you like.'

He strode off and she hurried to keep up with him. They took a path into the forest which was particularly dense on this island, and lush.

'You'll see some beautiful orchids here,' Craig told her. 'Keep a look out for them. Despite their beauty they are shy creatures sometimes.'

He saw the first ones, a spray of delicate pink-throated orchids, clinging high on the trunk of a tree, and later Rennie spotted others, some at ground level, some on the tree trunks. There were colourful butterflies darting from one exotic flower to another and sometimes a flash of wings that she was never quite able to identify as a bird.

Once Craig called her to look at something, and she found an enormous yellowish green frog, perched goggle-eyed on a fungus-decorated fallen tree trunk. He loped off leisurely when he realised he was being observed.

The track suddenly emerged onto a clifftop and Rennie, who had not noticed they had been climbing steadily, gasped as she took in the magnificent view now before her. They were about a hundred feet above the ocean, looking down across the bay where the seaplane was anchored, and along the sweeping curve of golden yellow beach with its lacework of creaming breakers perpetually foaming onto the sand.

'Isn't it fabulous!' she breathed, following Craig to the cliff's edge. 'This must be the closest thing to paradise there is.'

Craig laughed softly by her side. 'Scenically it certainly is, and hereabouts the people are still largely unspoiled, happy-go-lucky and generous, but in other parts of the South Pacific which are more civilised one sees the sad results of too much materialism with selfish greed creeping in like an epidemic.'

'Aren't you afraid the Andersons will bring it here?' Rennie asked, thinking of Theo's enthusiastic plans.

Craig shrugged as they sat down on the flat rocks near the edge of the cliff. 'There is nothing I can do. It will come, and I'd rather see the Andersons bringing progress than anyone else. Alan and Theo do have some ideals, and some common sense. They're not solely dedicated to making money, thank goodness. They genuinely want to improve the lot of the Tavalei's people while preserving their unspoiled surroundings.'

'Theo is certainly full of plans and seems to have boundless enthusiasm,' commented Rennie.'

'And he's a very personable young man to boot,' Craig remarked, rather archly.

'I hadn't spoken to him much before today,' Rennie said, adding boldly, 'I like him.' Then she voiced a question she had wanted to ask before but never had. 'How did you find the job of doctor on Tavalei, Craig? Was it advertised?'

He nodded. 'Yes. It stood out like a sore thumb from all those other dreary, stereotyped ads in one of the medical journals.'

'And fired your imagination?'

He looked at her steadily for a moment, his eyes slightly narrowed. 'I suppose so...'

'And now you like it so much you want to stay for good?'

'I think it's quite possible I will.' He paused, staring out across the sea. 'England has nothing for me now,' he said after a moment.

'What about your wife and children?' The words were out before she could stop them, and immediately her cheeks burned.

He turned to her, startled. 'Rennie—you know...'

'Yes, Craig, I know.' She held up her chin defensively.

'I always meant to tell you,' he said, in some agitation, 'I suppose Anna...'

'No, it wasn't Anna,' she said, adding quickly, 'It doesn't matter now, Craig.'

'How did you find out?' he asked in a flat tone.

She decided to tell him. 'Do you remember Mrs Quinn?' she asked.

He looked puzzled. 'Mrs Quinn?'

'She wasn't your patient,' said Rennie, 'but the woman in the next bed was—a hysterectomy. Her name was Mrs Bates. She told me you and Mrs Quinn knew each other. It was the day Mrs Quinn was discharged.'

'Oh, yes, I remember now,' he said. 'She was a bit of a gossipy type.'

'She told Mrs Bates about your wife and children,' said Rennie dully, 'and she told me.'

Suddenly he didn't seem to be listening. Then he leaned towards her, a look of anguish in his face. 'It never occurred to me you would get to know. Rennie, was that the real reason why...?'

'Partly,' she lied hurriedly, pride urging her not to let him think it had been her sole reason. 'But there's no need to talk about it. I'm sorry I mentioned it. It doesn't matter now, does it?' Suddenly she couldn't bear to hear his excuses now anymore than she could two years ago.

He was looking steadily at her, but he drew back a little and sat clasping his knees, his fingers so tightly enmeshed the knuckles showed white through his tan. 'No,' he murmured, 'no, I suppose it doesn't.'

Rennie felt a constriction around her heart.

'I presume the Andersons know,' she heard herself saying rather primly, whilst wishing she could curb her curiosity. She looked at him sharply, but he gave no guilty start, just looked surprised at the question.

'Yes, of course they know,' he said slowly. 'Alan Anderson interviewed me for the job. As he was in England on business, he undertook to interview candidates for the position. He's a sort of unpaid emissary for Tavelei on many occasions. Naturally, my personal history was relevant.'

Rennie felt she was floundering out of her depth. Only hurt lay on this course but she had to go on, to ask the ultimate question.

'Since you're out here alone, I presume that means you...you aren't together any more. You're free to marry now?'

His eyes met hers briefly and a cloud crossed them. 'Yes, I'm free now.' There was a long pause during which Rennie could hear her own heart beating loud enough to compete with the breakers rolling onto the shore far below. Then Craig said slowly, 'My wife died about eighteen months ago. My children live with my sister in Edinburgh.'

For a moment his words did not sink in, and then Rennie whispered, 'Dead...' For some reason she had not considered this obvious possibility. 'I...I'm so sorry,' she murmured.

He gazed at the sky. 'She had a brain tumour. It was a year after Mark was born. She had a lobectomy but it was not successful. She spent the last three years of her life in a mental institution. When I realised that our marriage was over—for a long time I wouldn't believe it—that there was no hope for her, I couldn't bear familiar surroundings any longer, so I left London and took the position at Whitehouse where no-one knew me. I didn't want constant reminders, it was bad enough visiting her...' His voice shook and almost broke, but he went on, 'I just wanted to close the door on that part of my life.'

Rennie, her throat constricting, longed to put comforting arms around him but did not dare.

'But Mrs Quinn said she knew you, she didn't say anything about that.'

'No. She didn't know. She was only an acquaintance, a woman I met briefly at a party in London. I presume she must have been living there too, then. I wouldn't have remembered her if she hadn't reminded me. She evidently chatted to Eleanor on that occasion. It must have been all of three years ago then. But I remembered the party, because that was the last party Eleanor ever went to. That was the night she started having dreadful headaches. I remember her saying how awful she felt trying to be nice to this garrulous woman...' His voice trailed away.

Rennie felt utterly stunned. Mrs Bates had given her a quite different impression, probably because the garrulous Mrs Quinn had not bothered to mention just how long ago and how casually she had met Craig. Rennie had naturally believed she was a current friend of his and his wife's.

'Why didn't you tell me about her?' she whispered.

He turned to look at her, sadly. 'I know I should have done. I'm not sure why I didn't. Perhaps I was ashamed to, it's difficult to rationalise something so deep seated. I didn't want your pity.' He unclasped his hands and smiled suddenly. 'But let's not be gloomy. I'm glad you know. I've wanted to apologise to you ever since we met again, but it was difficult.'

'To apologise to you.' That was all he had ever been going to say to her, Rennie thought bitterly.

He said again with some emphasis, 'Anyway, it's all water under the bridge and it doesn't matter now.'

Rennie felt the bands tightening around her heart. It did matter to her. It mattered terribly. Suddenly she was facing the possibility that her precipitate action, her cowardice and her pride, two years ago, might have cost her the love of the one man she had ever truly loved. He had not wanted her pity, he had said, but if she had asked him about his wife, perhaps he would have told her the truth and things might have been...suddenly her breath was dry in her throat and tears were burning her eyelids.

'My children are coming out in about ten days as a matter of fact,' he said. 'I thought it was time we got reacquainted, and my sister has enough to cope with looking after her own brood and our father. A few years out here won't do them any harm. There's a perfectly adequate school and the climate will do them the world of good after the pollution and grime of the city.'

And naturally you want them with you now you're going to marry again, Rennie thought bleakly. She tried to visualise Lilianne taking on a ready made family and failed. But perhaps she was prejudiced against the girl. Perhaps once she was married to Craig she would change. He must know what she was really like.

She glanced at him, loving him if possible more than she had ever done, aching unbearably because he was beyond her reach.

'Hey, you two, time to move!' Theo's voice broke the uneasy silence between them, and looking round Rennie saw Lilianne's brother striding across the clearing towards them. She and Craig scrambled up. 'They told me in the village you'd walked this way,' Theo said. He gazed around. 'Superb view from up here, isn't it?'

Craig said rather gruffly, 'Let's get going,'

and he abruptly set off, striding well ahead of them back through the jungle.

Theo walked with Rennie and whispered, 'What's up with him? Did he make a pass at you and get his face slapped?'

Rennie almost slapped Theo's face for suggesting it. 'No, of course not!' she retorted hotly.

CHAPTER EIGHT

'I admit I'm flabbergasted,' declared Peta, her eyes wide with astonishment, as she told Rennie about it. 'I just didn't think of him as being married. And now you say you knew all along!'

'I knew he was married,' said Rennie carefully, 'but I didn't know the whole story. He was, well, close about his personal life. I thought it was up to him to tell people so I said nothing, not even to you. I didn't know myself until yesterday that his wife had died in such tragic circumstances.'

Having put the children to bed, they were sitting on the verandah in the early evening, enjoying a few quiet moments while waiting for Brett and Andrew to come back from the yacht. Peta had just told Rennie how that morning she had learned about Craig's wife.

She had been watching him in the garden, through the living-room windows, absorbed in carving faces in some coconut shells for Damien and Emma. Their delighted laughter had brought Anna to her side to see what was going on, and Peta had remarked how wonderfully well Craig got along with children, and that it was a pity he didn't have any of his own.

Anna had said in surprise, 'Oh, but he has! Didn't you know?' And she had told the astounded Peta of Craig's two children, and his wife who had died tragically eighteen months before, after a long illness.

'You could have knocked me down with a feather,' Peta said, still stunned by the revelation. 'Apparently, he has a girl and a boy, like us. Jenny is seven and Mark is six. Anna is dying to see them. It's strange he never mentioned they were coming though, don't you think?'

'I imagine as we'll be gone by the time they arrive, he thought it wasn't necessary. It would have entailed explaining about his wife and that must still be a very painful subject.' She added, 'Also, he's not a man who courts pity.'

Peta nodded. 'Yes, poor man. I do feel sorry for him. It's why he sometimes looks so sombre, I suppose. He must have suffered terribly, all those years when his wife was ill. It must have been a tremendous strain. I wonder if he had anyone to share his troubles with, anyone to comfort him.' She sighed sympathetically and Rennie swallowed hard.

She was thinking of the long evenings he had spent at her flat, where he had stretched out in a chair, eyes closed, listening to music, just holding her hand sometimes. He had always said how relaxed he felt with her, how free from worries. She had never dreamed how terrible his worries were.

'Still, he seems happy enough on the whole, now,' said Peta. 'Tavalei seems to have captured his heart well and truly.'

'Not only Tavalei,' murmured Rennie.

Peta glanced quickly at her. 'You mean Lilianne? You think now he does mean to marry her?'

'Why not? She's young and beautiful and she's crazy about him. Mrs Anderson will welcome him with open arms, and Mr Anderson will help the hospital as much as Craig wants, I don't doubt.'

Peta's scrutiny was sharp. 'You sound as cynical as I was!'

Rennie had not meant that sharp edge to creep into her voice. 'I didn't mean to,' she said.

'I can't really believe he loves that girl,' said Peta thoughtfully. 'She's so self-centred and vain. What on earth can they have in common?'

'She's a nurse,' Rennie pointed out.

'Not a very dedicated one,' stated Peta

emphatically. 'I watched her sometimes when I was with Brett, and she never struck me as having the same interest in her work as any of the others in the hospital. She always seemed so bored, and as though everything was too much trouble. Now that pretty little girl, Jeanette, is a different person altogether.'

'She's also an excellent nurse,' said Rennie with warmth.

'As well as a first-class seawoman,' said Peta, as though the fact rather surprised her. 'I was impressed with the way she handled that yacht with Andy.' She laughed. 'So was he!' She paused and subjected Rennie to a thoughtful scrutiny before she went on. 'Andy's not the man for you, is he?' she asked bluntly.

'No, I'm afraid not. But he understands...' Rennie said quickly.

Peta nodded. 'Yes, he would. He's not one to waste his effort where there's no return, is my brother. Pity, though.' She smiled wistfully, 'I'd rather set my heart on having you as a sister-in-law. We get along so well.'

'I just hope Andy doesn't feel too slighted,' Rennie said. 'I wouldn't like any...er... awkwardness to spoil the rest of the trip.'

Peta shook her head emphatically. 'No, I'm certain there won't be anything like that. Andy is a good loser. He'll treat you as a pal if that's what you want.' She smiled wickedly. 'I guess you know that already, seeing you spent a whole night on Pudding Island with him!'

Rennie said doubtfully, 'I was only worrying in case he really is hurt. I mean. I could fly home from here if you thought I should.'

Peta considered this for a moment, then said with conviction, 'You mean, if Andy were really deeply in love with you, the rest of the trip would be intolerable for him? Well, that's a generous thought on your part, offering to quit, but believe me Andy isn't the kind of man to indulge in self-pity. He's the kind who'll fall in love deeply only if his love is reciprocated. Then, contrary to all appearances, he'll be as faithful as a bloodhound. He has deep feelings but he doesn't waste them, and I think I know my brother well enough to make that judgement.'

Rennie was glad to have her own tentative view confirmed by Andrew's sister. She had no wish to hurt anyone as she had been hurt herself. She said. 'I certainly don't want to leave you in the lurch.'

'And we don't want you to!' said Peta with feeling. She went on, 'Now you...you're different to Andy. If you fall in love, it's for keeps, come what may. Even if you married someone else, the one you loved first would always claim a place deep in your heart.'

Rennie flushed. 'You're an expert?'

Peta laughed. 'I majored in psychology!' She added, 'Seriously though, I'm right, aren't I? You've been carrying a torch for someone for ages, and until a very special man comes along and lights a bigger fire, you still will. Andy just isn't a big enough fire.'

Rennie smiled ruefully. 'Do you always sum people up so neatly?'

Peta grimaced. 'What you're trying to say is that I'm a dreadful busybody. Yes, I know it's one of my failings, but I like to know what makes people tick. Rennie, I'm glad it isn't you in love with Andy and he the indifferent one, because then I would have to pack you off home by air to save you months of suffering. As it is we'll have a happy voyage,' she laughed again, 'and Brett and I won't have to worry about playing gooseberry!'

With their sailing day imminent, Rennie began to feel more restless than ever. She was anxious to get away from Tavalei now, and to begin the slow process of putting the past behind her yet again. Somehow, she thought, she must be able to get Craig out from under her skin.

And then the unexpected happened. The day before they were to set off, Peta went down suddenly with a bad attack of influenza, much to everyone's dismay and her own annoyance.

There had been a mini epidemic of it on the island ever since the Regatta, and it was a particularly virulent strain. Craig ordered her to bed and threatened that if she didn't obey he would admit her to the hospital.

'Pneumonia is a complication with this one,' he told her seriously, as she lay pale and weak in bed. 'Ask Rennie. We've had two cases already. You're going to be in bed for a week at least.'

Rennie confirmed what he said.

'But we're leaving tomorrow,' wailed Peta. 'We can't delay any longer.'

'Yes we can,' said Brett, putting his foot down. 'If it was too risky for me to cut short my convalescence, it's too risky for you. We'll stay a bit longer. Another week won't make any difference now. And I can continue writing the first draft of the book. It won't be time wasted.'

Peta grimaced. 'You mightn't care, but Andy will be mad at me!'

Surprisingly, Andy was not put out in the slightest; in fact to Rennie it seemed he was actually quite happy about the further postponement of their voyage. At dinner that night, when Brett told him what Craig advised, he said casually, 'Yes, no point in taking any risks.

We've got a long stretch of ocean ahead. I think Peta should be quite well before we leave. After all, what's the hurry? You can get on with the book, Brett, as you say, and we don't have to be back for any special time, do we? In any case we can cut short our visits in a couple of other ports if necessary. We left ourselves plenty of leeway, remember.'

If Rennie was a little surprised by his ready acceptance of the delay, she soon discovered what she was sure was the real reason for it.

She went down to *Spindrift* a day or two later and was just going aboard when she stopped short. A smile spread over her face. Andy was there and so was Jeanette Raoul, in a patch of shadow near the companionway, and Jeanette was in Andy's arms, and he was kissing her. Oblivious of Rennie watching from the quayside, they drew slightly apart and even from a distance Rennie could see the misty-eyed look on Jeanette's beguiling little face. The wind caught her dark hair and tumbled it across her face, and Andrew brushed it gently back, bent his head and kissed her again. Rennie swiftly melted away.

Later, sitting with Peta, she told her about it. Peta nodded.

'I'm not really surprised. I noticed they'd been together quite a bit lately. Andy's always trotting up to the hospital on some pretext or other, or finding mysterious things to do at odd times—when Jeanette is off duty I imagine!'

'Perhaps you'll have her for a sister-in-law,' said Rennie.

'Do you think it might be serious?' Peta sounded doubtful.

Rennie shrugged. 'Probably not. Although Jeanette said to me ages ago that she wanted to travel. She mentioned going to Europe, especially to France. She speaks good French. Her father was French and they lived in Tahiti for a while. He's retired now and they live on Tavalei which is her mother's home island.'

'Andy speaks French well,' said Peta, warming to the possibilities. 'He loves France. He spent two years doing Mediterranean charters from Antibes before he went into partnership building boats with Brett.'

'Sounds as though they'll have plenty in common,' said Rennie, and Peta laughed. Rennie went on, 'I've invited her to stay with me if ever she gets to England, so perhaps she'll have an added incentive to save hard now.'

Peta stretched an arm out of the bed and clutched Rennie's hand. 'Oh, it's too bad. I wish we could find someone fabulous for you!'

'Now, wait a minute,' Rennie protested, laughing.

'I want to see everyone happily paired off,' confessed Peta. 'I don't like loose ends.'

'I don't mind being a loose end,' said Rennie. 'Don't worry about me. I'm perfectly happy the way I am.'

'Theo is a nice boy,' Peta remarked casually.

'Oh, Peta!' exclaimed Rennie. 'You are incorrigible.'

'He likes you,' said Peta, 'and you wouldn't mind a life in the South Seas, would you? I get the impression you are rather taken with Tavalei.'

'Not that taken!' said Rennie, 'and in any case Theo isn't the slightest bit interested in me.'

'How do you know? All he might need is a little encouragement. He's rather shy.'

'Well, he won't get any from me,' said Rennie emphatically.

Peta's eyes narrowed shrewdly. 'You're not, I suppose, a little bit keen on Craig?'

The question caught Rennie by surprise. Colour flooded into her cheeks. 'Of course not! Don't be silly, Peta,' she protested.

'I just wondered,' said Peta reflectively. 'You see a lot of each other, and there's a way he looks at you sometimes, when you're not aware of it, that makes me think he might...'

'I think you'll find he looks at all women in

the same way,' said Rennie shortly.

'He's rather an enigmatic individual, isn't he?' said Peta thoughtfully. 'He's the kind of man who makes you feel that you'd have nothing in the world to worry about if you were his woman, that he'd look after you better than anyone—and don't think I'm being disloyal saying that. Brett's my number-one man, and he gives me the same feeling. It's true, too. The children and I always come first. I get the feeling Craig's like that, but I don't know—he doesn't reveal much of himself, does he?'

'He's sensitive of other people's feelings,' said Rennie carefully. 'That's why he's a good surgeon and doctor.'

'I hope some of it rubs off on Lilianne if he marries her. That young lady could do with learning a few unselfish ways if you ask me.'

Rennie decided the conversation had gone on too long, and was touching on subjects she wanted to avoid, so she rose and said, 'I think I've tired you enough, Peta. You'd better get some sleep.'

Peta sighed wearily. 'I guess you're right. Oh, bother this rotten flu. I feel so wrung out.'

The delay caused by Peta's illness meant, Rennie soon realised, that they would still be on Tavalei when Sister Donaldson returned and Craig's children arrived. Part of her very much wanted to see the children, part of her wished she didn't have to. She was curious too about Lilianne's reaction to them.

Lilianne had recently become very lackadaisical, and was often absent from duty, always with some plausible excuse which Rennie was disinclined to believe. She evidently cared little for the fact that her absences meant others had to work harder to fill in for her.

Once, patience stretched to the limit, Rennie remarked on her increasingly frequent absences, and Lilianne, not unexpectedly, merely tossed her head in a superior way and said, 'It's all right with Craig and that's all that counts around here.'

Rennie decided that her relationship with Craig must be so cut and dried now that she was certain she could get away with anything. She felt annoyed with him. It was all very well to pander to Lilianne, but it was the other nurses who were suffering.

The day that Sister Donaldson arrived, Rennie felt stupidly apprehensive. She came in on the flying boat from New Zealand, bringing Craig's children with her. He had arranged for them to arrive from Scotland in time to coincide with her return, so that she could meet them in Auckland and accompany them to Tavalei.

But when Rennie saw the tall fair-haired women in her middle thirties, she knew a deep sense of relief. Sister Donaldson looked every inch the competent nurse, and she seemed to radiate efficiency and calm from the moment she set foot in the hospital. Craig brought her there, with the children, after he had met the flying boat, and Rennie saw the look of relief on his face. He was naturally very glad to have her back.

It was a bit of a surprise to meet her so soon, as Rennie had expected Craig to drive her home, but apparently she had been eager to stop off at the hospital first.

'This is Nurse Phillips—Rennie—Elaine Donaldson.' Craig introduced the new nurses, and then presented his two children whose hands he was holding while they gazed around slightly awed. 'And these two brats are Jenny and Mark.'

Rennie's hand was firmly clasped in strong feminine fingers as Sister Donaldson greeted her warmly.

'What a piece of luck you turning up so opportunely,' Elaine Donaldson murmured in her pleasant New Zealand drawl. 'Craig wrote and told me how well you were filling the breach. I'm as grateful as he is. It worried me dreadfully having to desert so precipitately, but I simply had no choice.'

'You certainly didn't,' agreed Craig, adding, 'I hope you're quite recovered, and that you haven't come back too soon.' He looked her over with a concerned and diagnostic eye. Elaine Donaldson chuckled.

'What a fussy man you are! I'm as right as rain, so you'd better look out. Sister's on the warpath again! I suppose Lilianne has been trying to run rings around everyone whilst I've been out of action.' There was no malice in her tone, only resignation.

Rennie did not speak, but Craig said offhandedly, 'She hasn't been quite herself lately. She needs a break away from Tavalei. But let's not stand around gossiping. Rennie, would you mind delivering Mark and Jenny to Anna for me? Tell her I won't be long. I'll just run Elaine round to her place. Oh, and tell Anna too, that Elaine will have dinner with us this evening.'

'Craig, dear, that is kind,' murmured Sister Donaldson. 'Thank you so much. It will help me to ease myself back into a working life.'

'We won't expect you to turn up for a couple of days at least,' Craig said. 'Rennie, fortunately, has been delayed for a few more days by the illness of Mrs Carmichael, and I'm sure she won't mind helping out a little longer.'

'Of course not,' Rennie assured them.

She took over the two children, who once away from the other grown-ups lost a litle of their shyness. Rennie asked them about their trip and said how brave they were flying alone all the way to New Zealand, and weren't they scared? Mark said he wasn't, but Jenny said, with childish honesty, that she was 'a bit'. Rennie handed them over to Anna who was as excited as if they were her own. The children seemed a little overwhelmed, but Rennie felt sure they would soon love the kindly Polynesian in whose sole charge they would now be.

The next morning Rennie was hardly surprised when she found Sister Donaldson on duty.

'I couldn't mope about at home,' Elaine explained. 'Oh, it's marvellous to be back. I feel as though I've been away for years!' She looked around her. 'I hardly know where to begin.'

Her hesitancy however did not last long. Like the efficient nurse she obviously was, she was soon back in full charge and even had Lilianne scurrying to do her bidding in a way Rennie had never been able to achieve.

Alone with Rennie in the nurses' room at coffee break. Lilianne said with smug satisfaction. 'You'll have to stop throwing your weight around now, and toe Sister's line.'

211

Rennie did not consider the remark worth answering. She made herself a cup of coffee from the urn and stood with her back to the room, looking out of the window. When she turned around to put her empty cup down, Lilianne was sitting with her feet on a chair contemplating her shoes.

More to empty space than to Rennie, she remarked, with a sigh, 'I'll be glad when I don't have to wear these horrible shoes any more. Glamorous they are not!'

'Nursing isn't supposed to be glamorous,' rebuked Rennie involuntarily. The girl annoyed her intensely, and refraining from responding to her more personal earlier remark had required some will power.

Lilianne inclined her head and a smile curved her pretty but sullen mouth. 'Well, I won't be slaving for a lot of lead-swingers much longer,' she declared with satisfaction, 'thank goodness.' She held out both hands and spread her fingers. She may have just been examining her finger nails, but to Rennie it seemed her gaze rested longest on her left hand—the third finger, perhaps.

'Aren't you going to continue nursing after you're married?' Rennie asked. Perhaps Craig was perceptive enough to have discouraged it, recognising that his future wife was not cut out for nursing.

Lilianne's head swung round and she looked sharply at Rennie. 'Married?' she echoed, sounding surprised. 'Who said I was getting married?'

Rennie bit her lip. She had spoken without thinking. They had not announced their engagement yet, but she felt sure Craig had assured Lilianne of his intentions. She said, 'With a ready-made family to look after, even with Anna to help you, I suppose you wouldn't have time for nursing as well.'

Lilianne seemed about to exclaim again, but instead she closed her mouth and turned her head away, almost shyly. After a moment she said, 'Who told you I was going to marry Craig? He didn't, I'm sure.'

'No, he didn't. No-one did. I...I just jumped to that conclusion,' Rennie said. She could hardly admit to eavesdropping on their reconciliation.

Lilianne licked her lips and shot Rennie a triumphant look. 'You're jealous!' she said, 'You'd like him for yourself.'

'Don't be ridiculous!' Rennie retorted, a shade too vehemently.

'You don't fool me,' said Lilianne complacently. 'It's as plain as day you're crazy about him—but you're crazy about anything in pants, aren't you?' She added venomously, 'But men like Craig don't marry girls like you!'

Rennie clenched her fists against her sides, resisting a strong desire to slap the girl, not for the first time since she had known her. But there was nothing to be gained from losing her temper now. It was better just to be thankful that she would soon be gone.

Lilianne went on sarcastically, 'Never mind, you've always got Andy, that is if Jeanette doesn't steal him from you.'

There was a highly charged atmosphere in the room for a few moments after that, then Lilianne rose and was about to leave, when something seemed to strike her. She turned back to Rennie. In quite a different tone, she said, 'Rennie, I'd rather you didn't tell anyone else about Craig and me. Craig might be a bit put out...it isn't official yet.'

The nerve of the girl! thought Rennie. Expecting a favour after all she had just said!

She answered shortly, 'It's nothing to do with me.'

CHAPTER NINE

Three days before their new sailing date, Rennie found herself one morning looking after Craig's children as well as Damien and Emma. Anna had gone to the food market for some provisions and Peta, now almost recovered from her dose of flu, was down at the yacht with the men.

The children wanted to go too, so Rennie took them down to the quay to look over *Spindrift*, with strict instructions to keep out of Andrew's and Brett's way.

'I wish Daddy had a yacht,' said Mark enviously.

'I'm going to make him buy a big one like this,' said Jenny, with the complete confidence of the very young. With her fair hair and dancing eyes she was an attractive child, Rennie thought, but even if she wasn't able to twist Craig around her little finger to that extent, there probably would be little he would deny her. Mark was a charmer in his way too, dark like Craig, and with his father's way of fixing his large luminous grey eyes on you for moments at a time so you wondered disconcertingly what was going on in his mind.

She said, laughing. 'Poor Daddy doesn't have much time to go sailing, you know, Jenny. He's very busy at the hospital.'

'He'll have more time when the assistant comes,' said Mark knowledgeably. 'He and Mr Anderson were talking about it the other day, when he took Jenny and me to see them.'

Rennie nodded. 'Yes, that's true. Perhaps he will have more time to play with you then.'

Craig had spoken enthusiastically to her and Elaine Donaldson about the same matter. He had been discussing the necessity of another doctor for Tavalei with the hospital committee for quite some time, he had said, and Alan Anderson had agreed to engage someone the next time he went to England, which he planned to do quite soon.

'You'll probably both have your work cut out when the extension is built,' Elaine had said, 'and we can accommodate more patients. We'll need another couple of nurses too, especially as we won't have Lilianne for much longer.' A fleeting expression showed that she was not sorry about that.

So she knows too, Rennie had thought. Naturally Craig would have told her he was going to marry Lilianne, before anyone else.

Elaine had laughed suddenly, 'Tell Alan to look for someone good looking and about my age, will you, Craig?'

Craig had grinned at her. 'I'll do that! Like to give me a list of preferred characteristics?'

'Oh, I don't ask for much,' Elaine had joked. 'Good looks and intelligence will do!'

Peta was down in the saloon checking over her stores and making a list of things they would need when Rennie and the children went below for a few minutes.

'Can I help with the shopping?' Rennie asked.

Peta shook her head. 'Not really. I haven't much to get because I was just about fully stocked up when I went down with this beastly flu.'

'Don't overdo it,' warned Rennie. 'You don't want to have a relapse.'

Peta grinned. 'I won't, don't worry. I'm dying to get moving again—although I've really loved it here. By the way, we're going to have a farewell party tomorrow night. It's the least we can do, Brett and I agree, when everyone has been so kind to us, and Craig in particular. We've decided on tomorrow night, so that we can have our last night free, and sober. We'll all need to get a good night's sleep so we can

217

slink away at dawn if the wind's right.' She sighed. 'It'll be hard leaving Tavalei, even though I'm itching to get on with the voyage. I'm almost glad Brett went down with appendicitis.'

'That's right, woman, your pleasures at my expense!' Brett appeared in the doorway. He looked at the four children and smiled at Rennie. 'Quite a little family you've got there!'

'Mark and Jenny like the idea of going to sea,' said Rennie, 'so any time you're looking for a replacement crew...'

He ruffled the children's hair. 'Next time we're passing through,' he promised, with a smile. He added, 'Tell you what, Andy and I will be taking *Spindrift* out for a spell this afternoon to check a couple of things. Like to come with us?'

There was no doubt about their enthusiasm and Rennie agreed to go along too and keep an eye on them.

'We're going to ask Daddy to buy a yacht and then we can sail to England to visit you,' said Mark earnestly.

'Good lad,' approved Brett, and with a wink at Rennie, 'I'd better drop a few brochures about Carmichael and Barker, Boat Builders, on the good doctor's desk!'

'Well, I'm off up to town,' said Peta. 'You

coming ashore, Rennie?'

'Yes, we're going to the beach next,' said Rennie. 'I'm going to give Mark and Jenny their first swimming lesson.'

They left Peta at the end of the quay and walked around the lagoon to a popular bathing spot. As the children ran wildly across the sand, Rennie smiled to herself. To Mark and Jenny, being on Tavalei was out of this world. It was like nothing they had ever experienced, and if the past few days were any indication, they were going to revel in their new life. But her heart was heavy as she looked at them, so carefree and happy. She just couldn't imagine Lilianne loving them as they needed to be loved.

Lilianne had several times given the impression that she couldn't be bothered with children, and she had ignored Mark and Jenny completely on the one occasion Rennie had seen her with them and Craig. Once, after assisting at a delivery, she had later remarked to Rennie that she couldn't understand why people went on having babies, it was such a painful and messy business.

Rennie had replied that she would probably change her mind when she was married. Lilianne had just shrugged and smiled in her supercilious way, but perhaps marriage would change her. Rennie hoped so, for the children's sakes.

'Okay, this is far enough!' Rennie called. The children came racing back to fall in a flurry of sand around her feet, squealing with delight.

'Gosh, you're brown all over, Rennie!' said Jenny enviously as Rennie slipped out of her beachcoat. She was wearing an orange bikini underneath which tended to make her look even browner than she was.

Rennie laughed. 'Don't worry, you two soon will be. Just take it easy for a while, though, so you don't get sunburnt. Bad sunburn can be very painful, and you don't want to end up in hospital, do you? Here, let me put some lotion on you.'

Both of Craig's children were pale skinned, but already the sun was making its mark and soon, Rennie knew, they would be as brown as the Carmichael children.

'Are we going to be allowed at the party?' Damien asked presently, when they had been in the water for some time, and had returned to the beach.

'I expect so,' said Rennie. 'For a little while at any rate.' She lay back on her towel and adjusted her sunglasses on her nose, content just to sunbathe while the children expended some of their surplus energy in building a replica (so

220

Mark informed her) of Edinburgh Castle. It had been a strange interlude, Rennie thought. Soon it would all seem like a dream. If it were a story, she thought ruefully, it would have a happy ending. Even in real life, it seemed unfair that Fate should have brought her and Craig together again by such an extra-ordinary coincidence, only to keep them apart. Her thoughts drifted idly in a rather melancholy way for a while until, warmed by the sun, she fell asleep.

She was awakened by a shower of sand falling over her, and Jenny squealing, 'Daddy!' as she dashed past.

Rennie sat up and look around. Craig was indeed striding down the beach towards them. His daughter took a flying leap into his arms, was lifted aloft and carried back on his shoulders. Both of them were laughing merrily. There was no doubt, Rennie thought, not for the first time, that Craig adored his children. And despite the long separation, they had taken to him again immediately. She felt very glad about that.

Craig unwound Jenny's arms from his neck and set her down. He dropped into a kneeling position beside Rennie. He was wearing a colourful island shirt over swimming trunks, and it was unbuttoned, falling open to reveal his broad brown chest only lightly sprinkled with dark hairs. Rennie felt an almost overpowering desire to wind her arms around him as Jenny had done.

She was glad when Mark called out, 'Daddy look!'

'Wow, what a super castle!' said Craig admiringly.

'It's Edinburgh Castle,' Mark told him proudly.

'Yes, I recognised it at once,' said Craig diplomatically, with a sidelong glance of amusement at Rennie.

'Damien helped to build it,' said Mark generously. 'He dug the moat.'

Both Craig and Rennie went to inspect the castle more closely, and to enthuse over its construction.

Then Jenny said, 'Rennie's teaching us to swim, Daddy. I did three strokes all by myself, and then I sank!'

'I did four,' said Mark, not to be outdone.

'Very good, both of you,' approved their father. 'You'll be swimming like fishes soon. What a pity Rennie is going away.'

'Daddy will teach you,' said Rennie.

'Daddy's too busy,' said Jenny, 'Aren't you?'

Craig smiled. 'We'll have to see. I expect I'll

find some time somewhere.'

'Lilianne swims like a fish,' put in Rennie. 'She'll teach you in no time.'

Jenny suddenly pursed her lips, 'I don't like Lilianne.'

Craig's eyebrows rose a fraction and Rennie looked away, wishing she had not spoken.

He said, 'Why don't you like Lilianne, love? I thought you liked all the nurses. They're always playing with you.'

'Lilianne doesn't play,' said Mark bluntly. 'She...I don't know, she's...' He couldn't find any words for what he felt.

'She doesn't like little children,' said Jenny in a prim voice, and with a perception, Rennie thought, far beyond her years.

Craig laughed. 'Perhaps she's a bit over-whelmed by you two scamps. You're enough to make anyone turn tail and run. You'll like Lilianne, I expect, when you get to know her better.'

'I like Rennie,' said Jenny emphatically. 'I like *her* very much.' She added, 'So does Mark, don't you, Mark?'

Mark looked a bit embarrassed as he filled a bucket with sand. 'She's all right,' he acknowledged, and gave her a cheeky grin.

'He doesn't like Lilianne either,' insisted Jenny. 'But we both like Rennie. We wish she wasn't going away. She's good fun, like Aunty Peg in Edinburgh.'

Craig lifted one eyebrow as he half smiled at Rennie. 'Any time you need a reference, you know where to come!' His tone was rather dry.

'Kids are funny,' said Rennie, as the four of them ran off again. She wished Mark and Jenny had not so candidly stated their preference. 'They'll get used to Lilianne in time.'

'I don't suppose it will matter greatly if they don't,' Craig answered, in a rather offhand manner.

The remark puzzled and disturbed Rennie. Surely he realised it was important for his children to like their stepmother. Surely it mattered to him that they might not.

He stretched out on the sand, hands behind his head.

'You've still got a few months voyaging ahead of you before you get back to England,' he commented.

'Yes.'

'What will you do then?'

'I don't know. I haven't really thought about it.'

'Perhaps the sea will be in your blood,' he said, adding pointedly, 'and you'll marry a seafaring man.'

Rennie did not answer. Instead she got to her

feet. 'What about a swim?' she said, feeling she could cope with his company more easily in the water.

That afternoon, Rennie took the children back to *Spindrift* as promised and Brett and Andy took them for a sail across the lagoon and back. Mark and Jenny were in seventh heaven, and giggled at each other in the two spare life-jackets which Rennie insisted they put on. Damien was in his element showing off his knowledge of sailing.

The next day Rennie spent her time, alternating between looking after the children, and helping Peta and Anna to prepare for the party that night. A vast amount of food was required to be prepared to meet Anna's standards and even she, placid though she was, became a little flustered by the end of the day.

Besides the food, there was Anna's special-recipe punch to be made in large bowls, and flowers to be picked and arranged. Anna had enlisted the help of a dozen young girls and their final task was to thread the leis which were to be given to each guest. Some of them, together with some young men, would also be giving a performance of island songs and dances during the evening.

'It's going to be a marvellous party!' enthused Peta, as she and Rennie took a final look around, and agreed that everything had been done. 'Anna is an absolute wonder!'

Brett and Andrew came in and sampled the punch, pronouncing it excellent.

'It's just as well we're not sailing tomorrow morning,' said Peta with a smile, 'because I suspect it's rather potent! Now, hadn't we all better go and change. People will be arriving soon.'

Rennie showered and washed her hair. It dried almost instantly—non-shrink, perma-press, wash-and-wear, Andy had laughingly called it the first time she had dunked it in a bucket on board *Spindrift*. All it needed was gentle pushing into place all over.

Her new dress was hanging on the outside of the wardrobe. It was one of the locally made ones she had bought in a flurry of extravagance. It was a hand-printed cotton, full length and slit to the thighs at the sides. The bare-shouldered bodice held up by a narrow silver-thread halter, flattered her slim but curvaceous figure. The pattern of vivid green, red, orange and blue orchids, hibiscus and frangipani flowers, intermingled with ferns and seashells, would always remind her of Tavalei, she thought wistfully, as she wriggled into it. She had put on a couple of kilos lately, she notic-ed, but the extra roundedness of her arms and

226

shoulders and her breasts suited her.

With the dress she wore a pale pink coral necklace and earrings, and pink sandals which she had bought in Tavalei. With her deeply tanned smooth skin glowing against the rich colours of the dress, she felt almost like an islander herself, although no-one on Tavalei, she thought with a smile, had her light-coloured hair. She applied a pale pink lipstick and a touch of lip gloss, then sprayed her neck and inside her elbows and wrists with perfume.

Peta knocked perfunctorily and walked in. 'Rennie! You look fabulous!' she exclaimed.

Rennie turned. 'And Brett's going to fall for you all over again in that!' she said admiringly. Peta's dress was a filmy blue chiffon, over a clinging satin slip, and very revealing. Rennie had never seen the tomboyish Peta looking so glamorous.

'Delicious, both of you,' said Brett, taking each by the arm a few moments later, as he met them on the verandah. He led them proudly into the living room where the guests were already assembling.

Andy came up to them and added his compliments, but there was a slightly apprehensive look about him, Rennie noticed, and during the next little while, as they were all talking to various people she saw that he was constantly looking around as though for someone who was not there.

Jeanette, of course! she murmured to herself. Jeanette was supposed to be coming. All the nurses were taking a turn on night duty tonight so that no-one should miss the party. But according to the roster Jeanette surely should have been there early.

Craig and Elaine Donaldson arrived a few minutes later, and soon after them the Andersons made their entrance. Lilianne looked stunning in a shimmering green dress, and she seemed in high spirits, talking vivaciously to everyone, laughing and joking. She did not, however, as Rennie expected, make a beeline for Craig and cling, but almost seemed to ignore him.

Rennie was unable to stop herself wondering anxiously, as she had before, how this shallow butterfly of a girl would adapt to being a doctor's wife. It was unlikely that island life would content her forever. She would surely soon be trying to drag Craig back to civilisation. Rennie remembered the contempt she had shown for her sensible nurse's shoes as she noticed Lilianne's flimsy, strappy sandals with spike heels clicking across the polished floor.

When she saw Theo Anderson standing a little apart, Rennie went over to him and stood talking to him until, rather to her surprise, Craig asked her to dance. One end of the long living room had been cleared to make a space large enough for those who wanted to dance and a band of local musicians was providing the music. Rennie felt awkward in his arms and wished he had preferred to dance as Lilianne and Andy were now energetically doing, a step apart from each other.

'Tavalei seems to have made you bloom in more ways than one,' Craig remarked, his eyes drifting over her exotically flowered dress, resting for a moment on the golden tanned swell of her breasts, before returning to her face. 'You look in positively blooming health tonight at any rate.'

It was a rather arch kind of compliment, Rennie thought. And apart from those remarks, Craig said very little. Rennie felt tongue-tied as she so often did with him away from their work. There was nothing she wanted to say to him that could be said.

She was relieved when the music stopped and Andrew came up and claimed her, thrusting Lilianne into Craig's arms.

'I haven't noticed you dancing with Jeanette,' Rennie remarked pointedly.

Andrew's face clouded. 'Haven't you noticed? She isn't here.'

Rennie glanced around. 'Isn't she?'

He looked hurt and disappointed. 'She said she'd be here early.'

Rennie drew him to one side away from the dance floor. 'Andy, you've been seeing a lot of Jeanette. Are you...beginning to care for her?'

He looked embarrassed. 'Rennie, I was going to talk to her tonight, seriously. I wanted to tell her...Look, she wants to come to England and she said you'd invited her to stay with you. I was going to tell her, well, that I'd like her to come very much—and soon.' He smiled slowly. 'No fooling, Rennie, I mean it.'

'Andy, I'm sure she's very fond of you,' Rennie said.

'She hasn't come,' he pointed out, 'so she can't be. You women!'

Rennie felt sorry for him, and puzzled too. Jeanette had been looking forward to the party. It wasn't like her not to come. And if she wasn't serious about Andy she was the kind of girl, like Rennie herself, to tell him so.

Rennie made a quick decision. 'Look, Andy, she said she was coming, so something must have prevented her. If you like I'll slip up to the hospital and if she isn't there, I'll check whether she's in her room in the nurses' quarters.'

He brightened. 'Would you? I can't think what I've done to upset her.'

'I'm sure you haven't done anything, and there's a perfectly good reason why she isn't here, but as you won't be happy until you know, I'll go right away.'

Rennie slipped away through the open french windows onto the verandah and made her way up to the hospital. The two nurses on duty said they had not seen Jeanette, so Rennie went along the covered walkway to the small accommodation building where several nurses lived in. She found Jeanette's room and saw that there was a light on, so presumably the girl was there. Puzzled, she tapped on the door. There was no answer until she knocked louder and then a faint voice answered, 'Who is it?'

'Rennie, can I come in?' Rennie did not wait for a reply, but pushed upon the door.

To her surprise Jeanette was sitting at her dressing table, all ready for the party in a very fetching red dress with a full skirt and narrow shoulder straps. Her glossy dark hair was piled on top of her head with tendrils falling each side of her face, and there were frangipani flowers tucked into the back of it. Seeing her first in profile, Rennie was struck with the beauty of the girl, but when Jeanette turned to look at her, she saw with dismay that the

231

young nurse had been crying.

'Jeanette!' Rennie exclaimed, closing the door behind her, and going over to her. 'Whatever's the matter?'

Jeanette's face crumpled and she burst into fresh tears, covering her face with her hands, and muttering words Rennie could not catch.

Rennie put an arm around her shoulders. 'Jeanette, tell me what's wrong. Andy wants to know why you aren't at the party.'

This provoked a fresh convulsion of sobs, and finally all Jeanette managed to say vehemently, was, 'I hate him!'

'Jeanette! What are you saying? Why? What has he done?'

Jeanette shook her head wildly. 'I don't know what to say. I've made such a fool of myself, and...'

'How? For goodness sake explain!' cried Rennie.

Jeanette made a supreme effort to control herself. Then raising her tear-drenched face, she said calmly, 'I don't understand how he could...how he could be so nice to me, when you and he...oh, Rennie, I didn't mean to encroach. I felt guilty all the time and I knew I should stop seeing him, but he kept coming, and I was weak. It's all my own fault.' She paused and heaved a deep sigh. 'Tonight, I just couldn't face either of you, because...'

'Yes,' Rennie prompted.

'Because I couldn't bear it!' Her large dark eyes pleaded with Rennie. 'I'm sorry, Rennie, I didn't mean it to happen.'

'Are you trying to tell me that you're in love with Andy?' asked Rennie.

Jeanette nodded miserably.

'Well, that's terrific,' said Rennie, 'because I'm pretty sure he's in love with you. He's like a cat on hot bricks back there at the party because you haven't turned up. He's sure he's done something to upset you.'

Jeanette's eyes opened wide. 'But you and he...'

Rennie smiled at her. 'Nothing. There's nothing between Andy and me.'

'You mean it's over?' Jeanette looked frantic. 'Because of me?'

Rennie chuckled. 'Long before you. It never really started. Andy and I are very good friends, that's all. I'm surprised he didn't tell you that. Although on second thoughts perhaps at first it didn't seem important enough.

'But...' Jeanette was frowning anxiously, 'when you first came here, you were always together, and...'

'We spent a night together on Pudding Island,' said Rennie. 'I'm afraid that little escapade did make people jump to conclusions. But I assure you, Jeanette, it was perfectly innocent.'

Jeanette looked faintly cheered. 'Then I wasn't...'

'Trespassing? No, never. And Andy hasn't been just fooling around with you. Do you think I'd have stood for that? Having him bounding from one pair of arms to another. Be sensible, Jeanette. Now come on, wash your face and put on some more make-up, and come up to the house.'

Jeanette continued to look miserable. 'I can't. It's too late now. One of the others is due to go off duty. I'll have to change and take over from her.'

Rennie took charge firmly. 'That you are certainly not going to do. You're going up to the party and Andrew, and I'll do your shift for you.'

'But you're not...'

'Not officially employed here any more, I know, but I think in the circumstances nobody is going to mind. Just mention it to Sister Donaldson, will you?'

Jeanette's face finally broke into a smile. 'I can't believe it, that it's really all right.'

'Of course it's all right. Now hurry up before Andy drowns his sorrows in Anna's excellent punch. You two have got a lot to talk about,

I fancy, before *Spindrift* leaves.'

Jeanette's face crumpled again. 'Oh, I wish...' Then she stopped. 'No, I mustn't. I must be sensible. If he really cares, he'll wait for me, won't he?'

'Yes,' said Rennie, 'and if I'm not mistaken he'll expect to see you on the wharf at Southampton when we return. Go on, fix your face and go and make Andy a happier man than he is at the moment. I'll find myself a uniform and change, and tell the nurse whose turn it is she can go to the party.'

As she changed into the familiar blue and white uniform which she hd taken off for the last time two days ago, thinking she would never put it on again, Rennie smiled wistfully. She wished she could be there to see Andy's face when Jeanette walked in at last. She wished she could see their happiness—or did she? She didn't begrudge them their happiness but she envied it.

Faint sounds from the party drifted through the open windows of the hospital, but Rennie doubted it would disturb anyone. There was no-one seriously ill at the moment, no-one requiring absolute quiet, and anyone restless would be sure to ask for a sleeping pill. Rather, she supposed, most of the patients, would enjoy the pulsating rhythm of the music faintly in the background, the subdued murmur of voices and laughter drifting through the screen of palms and hibiscus and frangipani that separated the house from the hospital. The island people were accustomed to noise and music and gaiety. It was a part of their lives. If only it could have become a part of her life, hers and Craig's together.

'Oh, stop it!' she adjured herself angrily, setting out to do the rounds of the wards. She had sent both the young nurses off to the party, and was now alone in the still, silent hospital.

After checking that no-one required anything, Rennie strolled slowly back along the covered-in verandah outside the main wards, which looked across the central courtyard. Moonlight was streaming through the trees and glinting on the fish pond in the middle of it, and the air filtering through the insect screens was pungent with night perfumes. Would she ever forget the perfumes of Tavalei, she wondered? Would her memory one day not be stirred by the sight of a hibiscus flower or a frangipani bloom? She doubted it.

She walked slowly back to the Duty Room and pushed open the door. She was inside and closing it behind her before she noticed him. Craig was sitting at the desk, toying with a pen, and Rennie's heart missed a beat.

CHAPTER TEN

'Back on duty, Nurse Phillips?' Craig said, rising as she entered.

He was not smiling and she was sure he had come to express his displeasure at her rather high-handed assumption of authority, which she had no right to do. No doubt Sister Donaldson was annoyed too, Rennie thought now, as she had every right to be. She had not given a thought to their reactions at the time, she had been too anxious to send Jeanette off to the party. Now, suddenly, she felt guilty.

'There...there was a slight mix-up,' she said circumspectly, 'and as I didn't want any of the nurses to miss going to the party, I offered to hold the fort. Things are very quiet tonight.'

He stood by the desk looking at her while her heart turned somersaults. She had wanted to avoid being alone with him before *Spindrift* left, it was too painful, and now here he was, and angry with her.

'I'm sorry,' she murmured, when he did not speak, but just continued to look steadily at her. 'I should have asked your permission of course, or Sister Donaldsons's. I had no right to take it upon myself...' She was trying to anticipate his rebuke because it would hurt so much to hear it from his lips.

He took a step towards her. 'I just had a very illuminating experience,' he said. 'A few minutes ago I went out into the garden alone for a breath of fresh air, and to get away from the noise, and I disturbed a pair of lovers in the shadows. Andy and Nurse Raoul.'

'Oh!' Rennie could not help the exclamation, or the swift surge of pleasure his revelation gave her. So it was all right!

'They were locked in a very passionate embrace and broke off guiltily. I was so outraged that I tore a strip off Andy.'

'You what?' Rennie exclaimed. 'But, Craig...'

'I told him I didn't think much of the way he was behaving,' Craig said grimly. 'That it was no way to treat a girl like you.'

'But, Craig, you don't understand,' Rennie broke in desperately.

'I do now. He told me. They both did. I didn't believe him at first, but Jeanette insisted you had assured her only minutes earlier that there was nothing between you and Andy. Is it true, Rennie?'

She nodded. 'Yes.'

Another step brought him very close to her, and before she could back away he had grasped her hands and lifted them, holding them tightly in his. 'You always gave me the impression that you and Andy had a very close relationship. Damn it, I saw you kissing him, and you spent most of your off-duty time with him...'

'And Peta and the children,' she murmured defensively.

His eyes bored into hers. 'There was plenty of gossip after the night Rolf Klein died, when you were gallivanting around the garden in your nightie! They said...'

'I know what they said,' said Rennie wearily. 'And it wasn't true. It was just Lilianne exaggerating.'

His grip tightened. 'You spent a night on Pudding Island alone with him,' he accused.

'We could hardly help that!'

His gaze was steady and penetrating. 'I found you asleep together, his arm around you, in the morning.'

She shrugged. 'I can't help what you think. We didn't have much clothing and only one blanket. It was quite chilly after the storm.'

He pulled her hands, still firmly clasped in his, against his broad chest and held them there. His eyes looked searchingly down into hers for a long moment, then he said slowly,

'Do you mean to tell me there was nothing.'

She shook her head. 'Nothing.' She lowered her eyes and murmured candidly, 'There was a time when I thought something might develop between Andy and me—he's a very nice person, and an attractive one, but...'

'Yes?'

'I knew I was never going to fall in love with him.'

'Was that certainty after you arrived in Tavalei?' he asked, speaking with great care.

'I suppose so,' she admitted.

'Perhaps it was because you realised you still loved someone else?'

She tried to pull away from him. 'Don't Craig, don't humiliate me anymore! Haven't you hurt me enough?'

He refused to let her go. 'Yes, and I'm sorry, deeply sorry. I always believed you ran out on me because you were tired of me, and because you wanted to play the field. The other day you said it was partly because you had found out about Eleanor. Was that true, Rennie, or was Eleanor the only reason. I want to know...'

'I've got some pride!' Rennie whispered. 'Let me keep it, can't you? Oh, what does it matter now? Yes, I broke with you because I was angry with you for deceiving me. No, I was angry with myself for being taken in, for giving

240

myself to you like a fool. I felt so humiliated, so... used. I didn't want an affair with a married man!'

'I knew that,' he said softly. 'I knew the kind of girl you were—that's why I fell in love with you. Rennie, I didn't tell you about Eleanor because I was afraid you would think an affair was all I wanted. I was afraid you would think it was just a "line" and I was trying to arouse your pity as a way to rousing your desires. I never meant to...to take advantage of you. I knew there could be no future for us the way we would both want, until Eleanor died, and although I knew that must happen sometime, I didn't want to think about it. She was very dear to me, but although she had already been dead to me for a long time, I didn't want to be unfaithful to her. But I couldn't help falling in love with you, wanting you so much it was sometimes unbearable. I knew it wasn't fair, and every time I saw you I had made up my mind to tell you about her and to end our relationship before it went too far, but I never could—I was too selfish and I needed you so much. I hated myself for deceiving you. I'm sorry, my dear. I deserved the way you treated me.'

Rennie almost wished he had not told her, it only made it harder to bear now. She took a deep breath. 'Well, as you said once, it's all water under the bridge. We've gone our different ways and there's no point in looking back and regretting things. I don't hold it against you, Craig. I truly hope you'll be happy in your new life with Lilianne.

His eyes flicked open wide, Lilianne? What are you talking about?'

'I know it isn't official yet,' said Rennie, trying again to draw away from him, 'but I guessed a while ago. Don't worry, I haven't gossiped, although I think quite a few people are expecting you to announce your engagement at any time.'

'I'm not going to marry Lilianne!' he exploded, letting go of her in his astonishment.

Rennie was completely taken aback. 'But only the other day she said...'

'What did she say?' he demanded in a voice of controlled fury.

'Well, she didn't exactly deny it when I let slip that I supposed you and she would be getting married soon.'

'And what might I ask made you suppose such a thing?' he asked.

Rennie bit her lip. 'Lilianne was fond of giving the impression that you and she...'

'And you believed her? I would have thought you would know better than that, Rennie.'

'But I heard you talking,' Rennie blurted. 'That day you were reconciled.'

'Reconciled? What nonsense is this?' He stared at her. 'When did you hear this?'

Rennie flushed. She had admitted to eavesdropping and there was no getting out of it. 'It was that morning after we had the…er…fracas over the medication. I was just taking some lists to the laundry and your office door was slightly ajar. I'm afraid I heard most of what you said.'

His eyes glittered. 'What did you hear?'

Rennie had never felt so uncomfortable. 'I heard Lilianne say rather tearfully that I had spoilt things between you and her and that… and that she would have an affair with you if you wanted. And you said I hadn't spoilt anything, that nothing had changed, and you told her to come and sit down and you would straighten it all out.'

Craig's breath was drawn in sharply, and he now let it out slowly. 'But you didn't hear what I said to her in the heart to heart talk we had? No, obviously you didn't.'

'I felt guilty for listening at all. I went on down to the laundry.'

'It's a pity you didn't listen,' Craig said grimly, turning away for a moment, and then back to face her, arms folded across his chest, 'because what had to be straightened out was Lilianne. I knew she had a bit of a crush on me, and her mother is definitely predatory, but I didn't realise how deep it went. I had treated it as a joke and offered no encouragement, which was all I could do, but it wasn't enough.

'I'm surprised you could even think for a minute that I would see Lilianne as a mother for my children. Heaven forbid! I wouldn't have tolerated her in the hospital if it hadn't been for her parents. The hospital's future depends a great deal on Alan Anderson's generosity, as the committee is always pointing out to me. If we have to carry his daughter, it's worth it so long as she doesn't do anything too drastic. She's a hopeless nurse, bone idle and careless, but it's not entirely her fault. She didn't want to be a nurse but her mother thought it was a nice respectable profession for her daughter, and no doubt hoped she would marry a doctor!

'When she blurted out all that which you heard, I had no alternative but to put it quite bluntly to her that I didn't want an affair with her, and I wasn't in the least likely to marry her. I'm afraid one has to be cruelly blunt to people like Lilianne. She hated me afterwards, and obviously she's been jealous of you all along. She's astute enough to have guessed how

I feel about you, and she must have determined to do her best to keep us apart. That's why she let you think we were going to marry, since once you'd gone, it wouldn't matter. Thank goodness she won't be here much longer.'

'She's going away?' Rennie was surprised.

'Yes. I knew I had to go further than talking to her. I approached Isobel and Alan as diplomatically as I could and persuaded them that nursing is not for her, and that she would be happier doing something else. She ought to thank me for it, but she won't! She's going to England shortly with her parents, and she'll stay on with relatives until she decides what to do. I am unkind enough to suggest it will be nothing more than finding herself a well-heeled husband!'

Rennie was utterly nonplussed. All her firmly-held assumptions were crumbling.

'And while we're on the subject of Lilianne,' Craig said, 'I suppose she lied that morning about the medications?'

'Yes, I'm afraid so.'

'It didn't occur to me until afterwards that you were shielding her. I'm sorry I blew up at you, Rennie. You can put it down to jealousy. I should have apologised.'

'It didn't matter.'

'It did. I saw your hurt, but I was too upset

with you for other reasons to take it back.'
He drew her unresisting now into his arms.
'Rennie, I have hurt you so much, so often,
even these past few weeks. Can you believe I
never meant to, that I've loved you all the
time?'

He bent his head to hers and touched her lips
with his. There was no need for her to answer.
It was some moments before either of them
could say another word, anyway. Rennie felt
a great sense of peace stealing over her as
Craig's lips moved gently on hers at first, then
with mounting passion as his hunger and long-
ing communicated itself to her and aroused in
her the same desires. Eventually he raised his
head and looked lovingly at her.

'And you ran away because of me?'

'I thought I could escape you, leave the
heartbreak behind, but it didn't work. You
were always there,' said Rennie softly.

'I ran away too,' he murmured, 'from two
tragedies so close together they were more than
I could bear. I had lost you, and then poor
Eleanor. I was consumed with guilt about both
of you, so I ran away too—and this was about
as far on this earth as a man could run—but
it made no difference, you were there in my
heart and mind all the time. When you turned
up in the flesh I thought I was hallucinating.

It just didn't seem possible. It was the answer to a prayer I hadn't even dared make.'

He laughed suddenly. 'I really am ashamed of myself. Although I was sure you didn't care I had to try and keep you here. That's why I asked you to help at the hospital, to keep you near me, and why I persuaded Brett to convalesce for longer than was strictly necessary. I thought you might have seen through me, but you didn't seem to. When it looked as though you were definitely all wrapped up in Andy, and I didn't stand a chance, I was insanely jealous. Then I decided I must accept it and not be churlish. It was my own fault I'd lost you.'

'I was puzzled,' admitted Rennie, 'but so far as Brett was concerned, I trusted your judgement implicitly. Oh, Craig, I never imagined it was because of me...' She fell silent in his arms for a moment, then she said, 'Perhaps running away was the right thing for both of us after all, since in the end it brought us together again.'

He hugged her close. 'Adrienne, my darling, we so very nearly didn't make it despite my unethical behaviour. Tomorrow is your last day.'

The realisation came like a lead weight on her heart. 'Oh, Craig, for a moment I'd forgotten everything except...us.'

'You can't go,' he said fiercely. 'I won't let you. The Carmichaels will understand.'

Rennie looked at him in anguish. 'Craig, I have to go. I promised I wouldn't let them down. I couldn't. I should feel so badly about it. They've been so good to me. It won't be very long, a few months, that's all.'

'A few months!' he exclaimed, 'I can't wait that long for you.'

'I'll fly straight back.'

'If I know Peta Carmichael,' Craig said, 'she'll insist you stay. She's a romantic!'

'And that's why we're not going to tell them,' said Rennie firmly. 'What else could she say? No, Craig, we mustn't tell them. I'm not going to put them on that sort of spot. It wouldn't be fair. I must keep my promise.'

He stroked her cheek tenderly. 'All right. But I shall will the winds to blow hard and strong, and carry you along at a record rate! I suppose there's one thing in our favour. Andy will be anxious to get home quickly if Jeanette is going to be there to greet him.' His lips moved tantalisingly on hers once more, but as she was about to lose herself blissfully in his nearness, Rennie suddenly jumped back.

'Craig! Of course...'

'Of course what, my lovely?' he murmured huskily.

'Jeanette, *she* can go with them! She can take my place and I can take hers. She's a better seawoman than I am anyway, and she and Andy will have lots of time to get to know one another.'

It was a moment before the sense of what she was saying sank in. When it did, Craig smiled broadly, 'Good grief, why didn't I think of that? It's the perfect solution.'

'Do you think Jeanette will be able to go at such short notice?' asked Rennie anxiously.

'I don't see why not. In the circumstances I think she'll make sure she can.'

'Oh, let's go and tell them right away!' said Rennie excitedly.

Craig slipped his arms firmly around her unresisting body. 'Not just for a moment, I want to make sure just once again that this is real.'

As Rennie lifted her face to his, there was an insistent clicking. She opened her eyes. 'Bother!' She glanced at the call board where a red light was glowing and a shutter was flicking up and down to summon attention. 'Number eight,' she said, grimacing. 'That's Mrs Barnett. She'll be wanting a cup of tea. She always rings for tea about this time, as though it's a hotel!'

Craig smiled into her eyes. 'Then she'll just have to wait for a minute, won't she!'

Rennie slid back into his arms without question. He was the one who gave the orders around here.

'Yes, doctor,' she murmured, bringing her lips to meet his.